They stood there, gazes locked, the tension so thick Adam could almost feel it crackling in the air between them…

Neither he nor Jillian had moved. There was a little more than a foot between them, the same amount of space since he'd taken that step forward, but it seemed to shrink the longer they stood there, as though they were slowly drawing together.

And suddenly the emotion that had been building deep inside him finally burst forth.

Want. Pure, raw want.

There must have been a change in his gaze. Adam saw the instant Jillian recognized it, her eyes flaring the tiniest bit. With surprise. With awareness.

Yet still she didn't move away. Still she stared into his eyes, hard and unblinking.

And the emotion radiating from her wasn't anger, either.

It would be so simple to step forward and close the meager space that separated them, to pull her hard against him, to crush his mouth against hers, to see if her lips felt as soft and supple as they looked….

KERRY CONNOR

THE PERFECT BRIDE

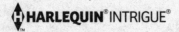

HARLEQUIN® INTRIGUE®

To Vanessa I., a good friend for so many years,
for showing just how much she still is.

Recycling programs
for this product may
not exist in your area.

ISBN-13: 978-0-373-74742-9

THE PERFECT BRIDE

Copyright © 2013 by Kerry Connor

This edition published by arrangement with Harlequin Books S.A.

For questions and comments about the quality of this book,
please contact us at CustomerService@Harlequin.com.

Printed in U.S.A.

HARLEQUIN®
www.Harlequin.com

ABOUT THE AUTHOR

A lifelong mystery reader, Kerry Connor first discovered romantic suspense by reading Harlequin Intrigue books and is thrilled to be writing for the line. Kerry lives and writes in New York.

Books by Kerry Connor

HARLEQUIN INTRIGUE

*Sutton Hall Weddings

CAST OF CHARACTERS

Jillian Jones—To solve her best friend's mysterious death, she had to go undercover as a bride.

Adam Sutton—The owner of Sutton Hall didn't trust the woman who arrived at the mansion to plan her wedding—and vowed to uncover her true motives.

Courtney Miller—She came to Sutton Hall for the wedding of her dreams, only to meet her death.

Meredith Sutton—Her idea to open Sutton Hall for weddings had taken a deadly turn.

Grace Bentley—Sutton Hall's longtime housekeeper considered the place her own.

Rosie Warren—The cook couldn't hide the cracks in her own marriage.

Ed Warren—The handyman was all smiles, but what lay beneath his pleasant exterior?

Ray Hopkins—The groundskeeper was a man of few words.

Zack Hopkins—The groundskeeper's son was a flirt who didn't consider any woman off-limits.

Prologue

She was going to be a beautiful bride.

Courtney Miller studied her reflection in the floor-length mirror and smiled. No matter how many times she tried on her wedding dress—and it was more than she'd ever admit—she couldn't get enough of how she looked in it. She started to run her hand over the skirt, only to stop and pull her fingers away at the last moment. At this rate, she'd handled the dress so much she was starting to worry she'd rub the satiny sheen right off the gown, and that wouldn't do at all. The dress had to be perfect, just as she would be.

Just as the whole wedding would be, actually. She'd spent the past week at Sutton Hall, the stately nineteenth-century estate in the mountains of Vermont, ensuring that it would. The mansion had just been opened by its new owners for weddings, and as soon as she'd seen the website she'd known she had to have her wedding here. It was a beautiful place, like something out of a storybook. She'd lucked out and managed to book early enough that her wedding would be the first one held here. That would only make it more special.

Tomorrow evening the rest of the wedding party would finally begin to arrive and the festivities would begin in earnest. And in just a few days she would be Mrs. Eric West.

In the meantime, though, she was still a single woman, she thought, meeting her reflection in the mirror, a slow smile curling her lips. She'd been reminded of that fact more than once over the past week, whenever her eyes had met those of Zack Hopkins, one of the groundskeepers here. The guy was temptation incarnate, with that shaggy dark brown hair, startling blue eyes and all those rough-hewn muscles. From the look in his eye and the smile that touched his lips whenever he caught her gaze, he knew it, too. The guy's obvious ego weakened his appeal a little, but damned if she could resist looking.

She would never do anything, of course. She loved Eric with all her heart. But some light, harmless flirting never hurt anyone. After all, she was still a free woman at the moment—

Bam!

The noise exploded in the room out of nowhere. She jumped, her heart seizing, her muscles tensing in surprise. Her hand reflexively flying to her chest, she whirled toward the sound.

The glass doors that opened onto the balcony rattled against the wind. Even as she watched, another gust hit them, shaking them so fiercely it seemed the latch could barely keep them closed.

The wind. It was just the wind.

Pulling in a deep breath, she eyed the doors warily. They opened onto a wide balcony that looked out over the valley. For anyone else it would probably be a magnificent view. Courtney had done her best to avoid it, the same way she did now. God, how she hated heights, she thought with a shudder. No one would catch her anywhere near that balcony.

The doors continued to shake under the force of the wind. Doing her best to ignore the noise, Courtney turned back to the mirror. The mansion had proven to be everything it was billed as. The weather, on the other hand, was not. It had been gloomy and overcast almost the entire time since she'd arrived. She was trying not to view it as some kind of omen. It was looking as though they wouldn't be able to take advantage of the gorgeous landscape for photographs. Fortunately, the manor's interior made up for it. There were plenty of places that would make great backdrops for pictures—

The face appeared in the mirror out of nowhere, directly over her shoulder, pure malevolence glaring at her.

She whirled around to find she wasn't imagining things. An intruder stood a few feet away, eyes dark with hatred, fists knotted in fury.

She couldn't even scream, shock seizing her throat and choking off the sound.

"Take it off." The words were snarled in a voice guttural with rage.

She could only gape in response. None of it made sense—the intruder's sudden presence, the words, the anger.

She somehow managed to find her voice. "What are you—? How did you get in here?"

The intruder lunged forward. "You don't deserve to wear that dress. Take it *off!*"

Hands reached out to grab at the dress. Recoiling, Courtney lurched backward, trying to get away from her attacker. She tripped on the back of her skirt and stumbled. Teetering on her heels, she struggled to regain her balance, throwing her arms out, flailing wildly.

Just as the intruder came at her again, hands thrust out, and shoved.

The push sent her careening backward faster, harder. She went straight into the doors behind her, the impact loosening the latch holding them shut and throwing them open. The wind burst in and grabbed at her as if with greedy fingers, grasping at her hair, tugging at the dress, stealing the breath from her lungs. The room seemed farther and farther away as she continued to stumble, lurching onto the balcony.

Terrified, she tried to find her equilibrium, recover her senses, see what was in front of her...

She didn't even realize what was happening as she landed hard against something behind her. She didn't register what it meant when hands closed around her and quickly lifted her off her feet.

She didn't understand until the last possible moment, when she was hoisted upward and propelled right over the edge of the balcony.

No!

And then she was plummeting, diving relentlessly downward, in free fall, faster and faster.

All the while the howling wind screeched in her ears, drowning out the sound of her own screams.

Chapter One

Jillian Jones had spent hours studying pictures of Sutton Hall, but she still wasn't prepared for her first glimpse of the place in person. One moment she was driving up the long private road that led to the estate, the next the trees framing the driveway suddenly cleared and there it was, the massive building looming in front of her.

She automatically eased her foot off the accelerator and stepped on the brake, bringing the rental car to a gradual stop. Her heart pounding, she stared up at the house she'd only seen in those photographs—and in her nightmares.

It was beautiful. In spite of everything, she couldn't help but recognize that much. The immense structure rose three soaring stories above the earth. Its gray stone walls appeared as solid and ancient as the mountains behind it and seemed to stretch as far. Each of its corners met at a round tower, giving it an appearance more like that of a castle than a simple mansion.

It was exactly as Courtney had described it, like something out of a fairy tale.

Unfortunately, as Jillian had been reminded all too recently, not all fairy tales had happy endings.

It was hard to believe it had only been a month since her best friend had come here to plan her wedding, believing she would have that fairy tale.

Instead, Courtney had left in a body bag.

Eric, Courtney's fiancé, was still inconsolable. This was supposed to be the happiest time of his life, and instead it had become the worst.

The guilt welled inside her again, bringing tears to Jillian's eyes. She did her best to choke back the feeling, but was unable to shake it completely.

She should have been here. That was the maid of honor's job, to be there for the bride. But she'd been swamped with work, having recently launched her own freelance graphic design business. After months of effort, she'd finally begun to build a client list and had projects she'd needed to finish. Not to mention the idea of dealing with flowers and dresses and seating charts had seemed like her worst nightmare. She'd even suggested to Courtney that she might want to choose someone else to be her maid of honor, someone who knew a lot more and possessed a great deal more interest in wedding arrangements than she did.

"It's a job for the best friend," Courtney had said. It didn't matter that they lived on different sides of the country and only got to see each other a few times a year, if that. Ever since they'd met in Mrs. Parks's first-grade class at Thompson Elementary, they'd been best friends, as good as sisters. "Don't worry, I won't make you do any girlie stuff. All you have to do is be there for me."

But Jillian hadn't been. The only thing Courtney had asked of her, and she'd failed.

Courtney had been alone here for a week finalizing the arrangements before the rest of the small wedding party was scheduled to arrive. And that was exactly how she'd died. Alone.

The official determination was that Courtney's death had been a tragic accident. She'd been on the balcony outside her room on a windy night, had come too close to the edge and fallen over.

Which was a load of crap, Jillian thought, the now familiar anger rising. Courtney had been afraid of heights. She never would have been anywhere near a balcony, let alone close enough to fall from one. But the door to her room had supposedly still been locked from the inside. There'd been no indication of foul play or any reason the police could determine why anyone would want to hurt her. In the absence of any hard evidence proving otherwise, the authorities had concluded it had to be an accident.

Leaving Jillian no choice but to come here herself and find out the truth.

She'd known if she came here as herself, it was unlikely anyone would talk to her or that she'd learn anything different from what the authorities already had. No, she'd needed another reason to be here. So she'd called pretending to be a bride wanting to book her own wedding.

Her main concern had been that someone would remember her name as that of Courtney's missing maid of honor. Luckily Courtney had always called her Jay—the only person who had—so Jillian knew if her name had come up at all, it would have been the nickname. The woman she'd spoken with on the phone—Meredith Sutton, one of the owners—had given no indication she recognized Jillian's name. She'd merely been cautious, wanting to be sure Jillian knew what had happened here. Unsurprisingly, it seemed that nearly all of the other weddings that had been booked at the manor had been canceled, their brides and grooms no longer interested in being wed anywhere near Sutton Hall. Jillian had assured the woman she was aware of the tragic death and wasn't deterred by the fact that such an unfortunate accident had taken place. Meredith

Sutton had still hesitated, as though she wasn't sure she wanted to try hosting another wedding here herself, before finally relenting.

Now Jillian was going to have to do all the things she'd shrugged off before—immerse herself in wedding arrangements, choose flowers and color schemes and whatever else was involved. For Courtney she would do it, the way she should have the first time.

And more important, she was going to get the truth.

Sucking in a breath, Jillian finally moved her foot back to the gas pedal and proceeded on to the house.

Unsure where to park, she rounded the circular driveway and pulled up directly in front of the building. The car had barely come to a stop when the front door to the house swung open. A woman stepped outside and stood on the stoop, raising her hand to wave.

This is it, Jillian thought, bracing herself as she put the car in Park. *Showtime.*

With one last deep breath, she climbed out of the car, fixing a smile upon her face as she waved back at the woman. Jillian recognized her from her research. This was Meredith Sutton, the woman who owned the estate with her brother, Adam.

"Hello!" the woman called out, a trace of a tremor in her voice. "You must be Jillian."

"That's right. Meredith?" Jillian asked as if she didn't know.

"That's me," the woman said, a touch of self-deprecation in her words. "It's great to finally meet you in person."

"You, too." Meredith Sutton was a thin woman in her late twenties with brown hair that hung to her shoulders. It was pulled away from her face, revealing pale skin and a faint smile. An air of vulnerability hung over her, as though a stiff breeze was capable of blowing her over. As soon as she made eye contact, her gaze almost immediately skittered away. A few seconds later, she managed to bring her eyes up again, this time meeting Jillian's and holding steady.

Jillian could almost feel the effort it took her to maintain eye contact. The woman radiated nervous energy. Considering what had happened to the first bride who came here to be married, that probably made sense.

Or was there more to it? Jillian couldn't help wondering as a pang of suspicion struck low in her gut. Something beyond a simple accident had happened to Courtney, she had no doubt about that. Someone was very likely involved, and as one of the owners, Meredith Sutton was more likely than not to know what had really happened here. Maybe she had good reason to be nervous. Guilty conscience?

Doing her best not to let her suspicions show on her face, Jillian leaned back and gestured toward the building. "This is so much more than I expected."

"The pictures don't quite do it justice, do they?" Meredith said, following Jillian's gaze. "I don't mean to sound like I'm bragging. Adam and I inherited the place almost a year ago and most days it still catches me by surprise that we actually own something like this. It's hard to believe a place like this even exists anymore as it is."

"Did you come here much before you inherited it?"

"Never," Meredith admitted. "We didn't know it existed. The last owner was a distant relative we'd never heard of. He didn't have any other relations, so the place fell to us. The whole thing was pretty amazing."

Jillian had to agree. Inheriting a place like this from an unknown relative was pretty incredible, and so was the place itself. Still, as she took it in from this angle, a sense of foreboding washed over her, sending her heart pounding faster. From a distance, with the sunlight shining down upon it, the massive structure had appeared majestic and regal. Standing this close, peering up at the building, it looked different. Gloomy. Oppressive. There were so many corners the sunlight didn't touch or that had long shadows cast upon them, the windows a thousand hooded eyes staring back at her. The house suddenly seemed as sinister as Jillian had thought it would be…and seen in her nightmares.

She wanted to believe she was just imagining things, projecting her own feelings on the building. She couldn't quite manage it, as a chill slowly rolled down her spine.

Meredith fluttered a hand, drawing Jillian's attention back to her. "Anyway, come in, come in. You've had a long trip. I'm sure you'd like to get settled in."

"Should I move the car?" Jillian asked.

"Just give me your keys and I'll have someone take care of that and get your bags for you."

The woman held out her hand for the keys. Jillian hesitated for a split second, suddenly unsure whether she wanted to be separated from her only means of escape from the place, the isolation and distance from the closest town hitting her. Still, there was no reasonable way to turn down the offer. Telling herself she was being ridiculous, she dropped the keys in Meredith's palm.

If the woman noticed Jillian's hesitation, she didn't show it, her expression never changing as she gestured for Jillian to precede her inside. "Please."

Pushing aside the last of her misgivings, Jillian worked up a smile and stepped through the entryway.

She'd barely made it over the threshold when she came to a stop, overwhelmed by the sight that met her eyes. Before her was a massive foyer that seemed to rise a full two stories. At the other end of the space stood a wide staircase that split in two halfway up and curved upward in either direction to reach the next level. A large glass chandelier suspended in the center of the room glowed golden beams downward. High archways on the sides offered tantalizing glimpses of the rooms and hallways beyond.

For a moment, Jillian's suspicions and her wariness of the place faded away, overshadowed by the reality before her. It really was magnificent, the kind of place it was hard to believe existed, as Meredith had said, or that she would ever find herself in.

"Takes your breath away, doesn't it?" Meredith murmured, stepping up beside her.

"It really does."

As she continued to take it all in, a woman entered from the left and came to stand in the center of the foyer, folding her hands in front of herself as though waiting to greet them.

Meredith automatically moved forward, leaving Jillian to do the same a moment later. "Jillian, this is Grace Bentley, our head of housekeeping here, though that title doesn't begin to cover what she does. Grace has been here at Sutton Hall for almost thirty years and has been in charge for most of that time. She knows the place like the back of her hand, far better than I do, and she'll be able to help you with any questions you might have, any logistical issues in terms of locations for wedding events, that sort of thing."

"It's a pleasure to meet you, Grace," Jillian said.

"Likewise," the woman returned with almost imperial formalness. "If there's anything you require, please let me know."

The words were polite, but there was no real warmth in them, and Grace Bentley didn't seem particularly welcoming, giving off a distinctly chilly air. She was a tall, thin woman in her fifties, dressed in a plain black dress, her dark hair tied back in a rather severe twist. She smiled faintly when she made the offer, her face a carefully composed mask that revealed nothing.

"Why don't I show you to your room?" Meredith suggested. "I know you've been traveling all day and might want to get settled in a bit before we jump in to the wedding preparations."

"That sounds great," Jillian said, meaning it.

After flying in from San Francisco, she'd had to drive over an hour to reach the small town of Hawthorne, Vermont, at the base of the mountain before continuing on to the manor. As eager as she was to begin asking questions and feeling her way around here, having a moment to take a breath and get her bearings would be more than welcome.

"Right this way."

They walked down the long red carpet in the middle of the marble floor toward the stairs, allowing Jillian a better view of something she'd noticed from the far side of the foyer, but had been unable to examine closely. A portrait hung at the juncture of the staircase where it split in separate directions. A man and woman in wedding attire—clearly a bride and groom—posing in this very hall. They were smiling, understandably enough, and the artist had managed to capture the glow of happiness on their faces so well Jillian could hardly imagine a photograph showing it better.

Judging from the style of the wedding dress, which was pretty but of a fashion several decades older, the portrait had clearly been hanging there for some time. Seeing it, Jillian had no trouble understanding why Meredith had been inspired to open the place for weddings.

Then she thought of Courtney and Eric and

how happy they had been, how happy they *would* have been on their wedding day, one that would never take place.

"This is the last owner of Sutton Hall, Jacob Sutton, and his wife, Kathleen, on their wedding day," Meredith explained, a touch of wistfulness in her voice.

"What happened to them?" Jillian asked. This was one area she didn't know much about, not having done much research on the previous owners.

"Sadly she passed away five years later. A car accident. The vehicle she was driving went off the road on the way up the mountain during a storm."

Looking at the woman's smiling face, Jillian felt a twinge of sadness. She'd been so happy. She'd had no idea what the future held for her. Just like Courtney.

"And him?"

"He continued living here at Sutton Hall the rest of his life. He never remarried, never really got over losing her. Right, Grace?"

The woman didn't respond, and Jillian wondered if she was even there anymore. She glanced back to find the housekeeper standing a few yards behind them, her steady gaze fixed on the portrait.

No, Jillian thought, not just on the portrait,

but on the face of Jacob Sutton, her eyes burning with an unreadable, but intense look.

As if realizing that she hadn't answered—or that Jillian was watching her—Grace met Jillian's gaze before slowly lowering her eyes. "That's right."

Returning her attention to the painting, Meredith let out a little sigh. "They may have only had five years together, but evidently they were happy ones. And afterward, he loved her so much he never thought of being with anyone else."

How sad, Jillian thought at the idea of the man living alone in this massive house for all those years. Though from the way Meredith had told the story, she had the feeling that wasn't the response she was supposed to have. She managed to say, "How romantic."

"Or depressing."

The comment echoing her own thoughts was the last thing Jillian expected to hear, and she turned her head in surprise. The statement hadn't come from Meredith, but from a masculine voice above them.

A man was striding down the stairs toward them, his eyes unmistakably pinned on her. He walked with an easy, confident grace, taking his time in both his approach and his study of her. He moved like he owned the place, very "Lord of the Manor."

Which was exactly who he was, of course.

Adam Sutton.

Jillian recognized him, too. But like the mansion he and his sister owned, the man made a much larger impression in person than his photographs could begin to show.

He was a tall man in his mid-thirties, his body demonstrating a muscled leanness beneath the black pullover and slacks he wore. He was undeniably good-looking, with thick black hair and high cheekbones, though perhaps not conventionally handsome. His features were too hard, too sharp, too intense. But more than that, there was something utterly compelling about him that immediately grabbed her attention and refused to let go, every instinct in her body—good and bad—instantly going on alert. Everything about him projected confidence bordering on arrogance. Meeting his dark, steady gaze, she found herself helpless to look away.

Jillian knew from her research that he'd been a management consultant before giving it up to take over Sutton Hall and open it for weddings with his sister. It seemed a strange choice for the man before her to have made. She couldn't imagine him being remotely interested in weddings. On the other hand, just looking at him, Jillian had no doubt he'd been successful in the business world.

The man would be a formidable adversary. And from the way he was looking at her, she suspected that was exactly what he was to her.

Doubt flickered for an instant, and she wondered if he knew who she was....

She'd find out soon enough.

"Adam!" Meredith called as he joined them on the landing. "Jillian, this is my brother, Adam," Meredith said. "Adam, Jillian Jones."

"Welcome to Sutton Hall," he said, his mouth curving slightly in what might have passed for a smile.

"Thank you. It's great to be here."

"Is it?" he returned, the smile deepening as though he'd caught her in a trap. "After the recent events I'm sure you've heard about, most women planning their weddings wouldn't want to be anywhere near here. It seems only natural. Yet here you are."

"Adam," Meredith murmured in admonition under her breath.

"You're right," Jillian said without taking her eyes from the man. "I'm sure most people would be put off getting married somewhere a bride-to-be so recently died."

"But not you?" he said with a slightly mocking note in his voice.

"No," Jillian said. "I don't believe in bad luck

or omens. I believe in myself." That much was certainly true.

"You must, since you came here by yourself," he pointed out. "You didn't want to bring anyone else from the wedding party to help you with the arrangements?"

"Unfortunately, no one else could come with me on such short notice. I'm going to have to try to get everything organized on my own."

"Neither your fiancé nor any of your family and friends had any problem letting you come here by yourself?"

"They know I can take care of myself."

"I suppose you'll have to."

"No, you won't," Meredith interjected. "You'll have everyone at Sutton Hall at your disposal to make this the wedding of your dreams."

Jillian barely heard her, her focus squarely on Adam Sutton. "I thought what happened to that poor woman was an accident. Is there some reason I shouldn't want to be married here, Mr. Sutton?" Jillian asked, unable to keep the challenge from the question.

He hesitated for only a moment, his eyes narrowing slightly, before replying. "Not at all, Ms. Jones," he said, something in his tone utterly unconvincing. "Not at all."

"Then there shouldn't be a problem."

"I hope not," he said mildly. It was an odd

response. As the owner of Sutton Hall and partner in the wedding business his sister had started, he should be reassuring her, shouldn't he, wanting to keep her here? But there was nothing reassuring in his words. Instead, combined with the way his eyes seemed to bore through her, his comments seemed to contain a message she couldn't quite decipher.

"I was going to show Jillian to her room," Meredith said into the silence that fell between them, the nervousness in her voice indicating she'd picked up on the tension between them. Not that there was any way anyone could have missed it.

"That sounds like a good idea," Adam Sutton said dispassionately, never taking his eyes off Jillian.

"Right this way," Meredith said, starting up the stairs.

It was a clear cue for Jillian to follow her. Instead, she remained where she was, her gaze locked with Adam Sutton's. Was he trying to scare her? Warn her? Was it possible he knew who she was? But if he did, why wouldn't he have exposed the truth and refused to let her come here? Or was this a trap, and he'd purposely brought her here to guide her to the answers he wanted her to have—or prevent her from asking the questions at all?

Peering up into the man's cool exterior and bottomless dark eyes, she found the last possibility entirely too easy to believe.

Finally realizing how long she'd been standing there—far too long to remain without having to explain herself—Jillian raised her chin and moved to join his sister.

ADAM WATCHED JILLIAN Jones follow Meredith up the staircase, his eyes briefly drifting to her gently swaying hips before he caught himself and returned his gaze to the center of her back. She was an attractive woman, there was no denying it. A slim blonde with startling green eyes and curves in all the right places, he would have to be blind not to notice.

Not that he had any business noticing. The woman was getting married.

Or so she said.

He was no more convinced about that than he was about her motives for being here, or anything else about her for that matter, as he continued studying her.

He wasn't surprised when she paused and glanced back at him as if she'd sensed his attention. Her eyes met his, one brow raising in silent question.

The polite thing would have been to look away, pretend that he hadn't been watching her.

He simply stared back, unwavering, unrepentant. Let her know he'd been watching, the same way he would be as long as she was here.

She frowned, her brows knitting together, and turned to continue up the stairs.

He should have looked away, he admitted. It wasn't as though he was trying to scare her.

Or maybe he was. Maybe she was someone who needed to be scared off, someone who was here to cause trouble. It was certainly easier to believe than the idea that she'd come here to be married. What kind of woman would want to have her wedding in a place where another bride had died so recently?

For Meredith's sake, he wanted to be grateful for this woman's presence here and apparent lack of superstition. But he didn't have that much faith in people, and Meredith had already paid once because he hadn't done a good enough job looking out for her. He wasn't going to let it happen again. If the woman was lying, Meredith was the one most likely to be hurt.

Grim determination settled over him as he watched the women reach the next level and disappear from view.

Every instinct told him Jillian Jones was going to be trouble.

And he was fully prepared to do whatever was necessary to prevent her from causing it.

Chapter Two

"Here we are," Meredith declared with a cheerfulness that was starting to sound forced. "I think you'll be pleased. This is one of the largest rooms in the house, with its own private bathroom, and it has a wonderful view." Pushing the door open and reaching in to flip on the lights, she stepped aside to let Jillian enter first.

The room she'd led Jillian to was on the second floor in the east wing near the front of the manor. Courtney had been staying in one of the tower rooms, Jillian knew, the one at the top of the tower at the other end of the east wing. Jillian had to believe it was nicer and had an even better view since it had been given to the first bride to come to Sutton Hall, but considering what had happened to that bride, Jillian could understand why Meredith had chosen differently for her.

Even so, it took only one glimpse of the room to prove Meredith had given her little reason to complain. The suite was every bit as nice as she'd said. A glorious four-poster bed stood against the right wall. Plush rugs covered the floors, and while there may not have been a balcony, the windows offered stunning views of the mountains, flooding the room with sunlight.

"It's lovely," Jillian said to the woman's expectant silence, not having to fake the admiration in her voice.

"I'm glad you like it," Meredith said with obvious pleasure.

"Is anyone else staying nearby?"

"Adam and I are both at the end of the hall, far enough that you should have privacy, but close enough if you need us."

"Great." It would have been better for her purposes if there was no one remotely close by, but that was probably too much to expect. Given what had happened to Courtney, they likely wanted to keep a closer eye on their guests during their time here. It was just another challenge she'd have to deal with.

"I thought we could meet in a little while to begin going over the plans," Meredith said. "I have plenty of ideas and options to show you, and of course I want to know everything you're thinking of. And Rosie, our cook, is ready to go over potential menus with you."

Jillian did her best to look properly enthused. Faking excitement for the wedding plans would be the hardest part of her mission here, hands down. "I can't wait. Just give me some time to freshen up and I'll be raring to go."

"Wonderful," Meredith said. "Well then, I'll give you a chance to settle in."

Mustering a smile, Jillian tried not to let her relief show. Truth be told, the woman's nervous chatter was beginning to wear on her nerves. "That would be great, thanks."

"Welcome to Sutton Hall," Meredith said, then turned and walked to the door, gently closing it behind her.

As soon as the door was shut, Jillian released a long, slow breath and sagged onto the bed. Shoulders slumping, she surveyed her opulent surroundings.

She'd done it. She was here.

That was the easy part.

Now she had a mystery to solve.

ALONE AT LAST.

Lowering himself into the desk chair, Adam savored the silence that surrounded him. When he'd first arrived at Sutton Hall, the room that had served as Jacob Sutton's study had been a disaster, packed with so much paper and clutter he'd barely been able to move through the space. Clearly Jacob had let things get away from him over the years. It had taken almost a full year, but Adam had managed to get the space in order. The study finally felt like his, a private sanctuary that offered a welcome place to retreat into his thoughts for a while. In the past month he'd needed that more than ever.

A brisk knock on the door suddenly interrupted the silence, the noise pulling a sigh from his lungs. So much for that.

He'd barely glanced up before the door opened and Meredith stepped into the room.

"Hey there," he said, his irritation fading. "She all settled in?"

"I think so. I asked Zack to move her car to the garage and bring her bags in."

Adam frowned. "I could have done that."

"I know. I was going to ask you, but I wasn't sure I wanted you interacting with her again so soon." She folded her arms over her chest and matched his frown. "What was that out there?"

"What was what?"

Meredith shot him a pointed look. "You know what I'm talking about. You weren't exactly laying out the welcome mat. You were practically interrogating her."

"Maybe she needs to be interrogated," he murmured.

Her frown deepened. "Do you really believe that?"

Adam released a frustrated sigh. "I don't

know. I just think it's very strange that this woman showed up so soon after what happened to Courtney Miller, has no problem having her wedding here and came here alone, the same way Courtney did. That doesn't strike you as odd?"

"Maybe a little," she admitted faintly. "After Courtney died, I thought we'd need a miracle to keep going. Maybe this is the one we need."

Regret shot through him, not for the first time, in the face of his sister's open vulnerability. He hated being the one to challenge her hopes that this could all still work out, but he had to be realistic, for both of their sakes. "Maybe," he hedged, no doubt sounding as certain as he felt about the possibility that miracles existed, or that they would be lucky enough to be granted one.

"You said you were going to look in to her," Meredith pointed out.

"I did."

"And what'd you find?"

He hesitated before grudgingly admitting, "Nothing. She seems to be exactly who she claims to be." Jillian Jones was a graphic designer who lived in San Francisco. Up until six months ago, she'd worked at a large advertising agency. She'd recently started her own freelance business that was just getting off the ground. She wasn't a reporter or an investigator of some kind, someone he could imagine wanting to come here to stir up the mess surrounding Courtney Miller. The woman's loved ones had understandably raised a fuss over her death, despite the fact that it had been a tragic accident, and he'd had to consider the possibility someone might come here acting on their behalf. That didn't appear to be the case, but that still left the possibility she could be some kind of morbid ghoul who got her kicks out of tragic events. Either way, it would be trouble they didn't need—which was exactly what his gut was telling him she was.

"Well, then what more do you want?" Meredith asked.

"For this to feel right, and it doesn't."

"I think you're just being overly cautious," she said. "Which you have every right to be after what happened. But maybe it's time things started going our way. Her wedding is our second chance to make this work. If it doesn't, we're not going to get a third one."

"I know," he said gently. "And I want this to work as much as you do."

"Do you?"

"Yes." *No,* he thought, because no one could want this to work as much as she did. The only reason he cared about this wedding business was because it mattered so much to her. It was why he'd left his job to dedicate his time and energy to making this work with her—for her. The idea to open Sutton Hall for weddings was the first spark of interest she'd shown in anything after what had gone down with that bastard Brad. This was her dream, and he was determined to see that dream come true.

And if Jillian Jones did anything to mess with it—with any of them—she'd answer to him.

JILLIAN HAD JUST stepped out of the bathroom adjoining her bedroom when she heard a knock on the door to the suite.

Moving to the door, she opened it. An incredibly handsome young man stood on the threshold, holding her bags. For a moment, Jillian was actually taken aback by how attractive he was. Dressed in jeans and a flannel shirt, it was as if he'd stepped out of a magazine ad depicting the prototypical outdoorsman, with thick dark brown hair, deep blue eyes and chiseled features.

And yet, staring into his perfect face, she felt none of the impact she'd experienced just a short time earlier when taking in Adam Sutton's entrance. Just the thought of the man sent a shiver trembling through her again.

As her eyes met the newcomer's, she caught the gleam in his. Oh, yes, he was very good-looking. And he knew it.

"Hi, I'm Zack," he said, flashing her a row of perfect, gleaming teeth. "I brought your bags."

"Of course." She stepped out of the doorway to allow him access to the room. "Thank you so much. I hope it wasn't too much trouble."

"Not at all."

He walked past her and set the bags on the floor at the end of the bed, then turned back to face her. "There you go. Anything else I can do?"

"I don't think so."

"Well, if there is, you be sure to let me know."

"I'll keep that in mind. So what is it you do around here when you're not helping women with their bags?"

"I'm one of the groundskeepers. Just started. My dad's the main one, has been for as long as I can remember. He's in charge of maintaining the property, especially the gardens on the east side."

"So it's kind of the family business?"

He wrinkled his nose, making it clear what he thought of that idea. "God, I hope not. I'm just doing it for the time being."

"I take it you don't enjoy it?"

"It's all right. Pays the bills." He grinned. "And it's gotten better now that I get to meet some interesting people."

She wondered for a moment if she was mistaking the flirtatious note she heard in his voice. It was possible he was only being friendly.

"Oh, I almost forgot." He reached into the

front pocket of his shirt and pulled out her keys. "I moved your car to the garage."

"Thanks. And where is that?"

"Around the west side of the house. I can show you if you like."

"That's all right. I'm sure I don't need to know right now." At least she hoped. And if the time came she did need to get to her vehicle quickly, she'd find it herself.

She reached out to take the keys. He dropped them into her hand, his fingertips grazing her palm a little too long. Warily, she lifted her eyes to his. He winked, that slow, slight grin curling one corner of his mouth.

Nope, definitely not imagining things. It was all Jillian could do not to roll her eyes. As far as the man knew Jillian was an engaged woman here to get married, and he was flirting with her? *Classy.*

"Thanks again," Jillian said, giving him the cue to leave.

"Sure thing. I'll be seeing you around." He walked to the door, an unmistakable swagger in his step.

Jillian barely had the door shut behind him before she gave in to the eye roll he so desperately deserved. Only then did the larger implications of his behavior occur to her.

A man with so few scruples he'd put the moves

on a complete stranger he knew was getting married likely wasn't someone to be trusted. She wondered if he'd made a move on Courtney. Jillian had no doubt Courtney wouldn't have acted on it, no matter how good-looking she might have thought he was. She'd loved Eric. How would Zack have reacted to being turned down?

Somehow Jillian suspected she was going to have to find that out herself. She would have to keep an eye on him.

With a sigh, she turned back to put her bags away. This was such a strange place with an… interesting group of people working here. She could hardly wait to meet the rest of them.

"AND IF YOU see what I did with the frosting here, it's another option that I think is quite lovely…."

Jillian had never thought she would get sick of looking at cakes. But then, she'd never seen Rosie Warren's album of all the cakes she'd made.

Jillian nodded and made a sound of agreement in her throat to make the woman think she was listening. She really didn't want to hear any more about cakes. At the moment she couldn't imagine ever wanting to eat one again.

Instead, she did her best to study the woman without making it obvious she was doing so. The longtime cook at Sutton Hall, Rosie was a sturdy-looking woman who appeared to be in her late fifties or early sixties, with gray hair and a rounded face and figure that gave her a grandmotherly appearance. She seemed pleasant enough, but Jillian wasn't getting much of a read on her personality, other than that she was exceedingly competent at her job. From the moment she'd sat down at the massive dining room table with Jillian and Meredith, she'd opened the album and talked about nothing but cakes.

When Rosie started to turn the page, Jillian quickly interjected. "This is all very impressive. You made all of these cakes just to have photographs of them?" She wasn't exaggerating. The album contained photographs of at least four dozen fully decorated cakes, something Jillian couldn't imagine her having on hand before Sutton Hall had been opened for weddings. For her to go to that much trouble was certainly impressive.

"Yep. Just like the professionals," Rosie said with unmistakable pride.

"Although if you'd feel more comfortable hiring a professional baker, we'd understand," Meredith said. "I do have the numbers of several in the area who come highly recommended."

"I'm perfectly capable of baking and decorating a beautiful wedding cake," Rosie interjected before Jillian could respond, her voice suddenly tight with anger. "I think my work speaks for itself."

"It certainly does," Jillian said. "I'll leave the cake in your capable hands. I trust you're more than up to it."

Rosie nodded firmly. "Thank you. So why don't you tell me what you have in mind when it comes to flavors, and I can prepare some samples for you to try."

Jillian was saved from answering when a door across the table from them suddenly swung open. "Rosie? You around?"

Moments later, a man stepped through, coming to an abrupt stop as soon as he spotted them. "Oh. Sorry to interrupt."

"It's no trouble," Meredith said. "Jillian, this is Rosie's husband, Ed. I'm sure you'll be seeing him around. He's our handyman and all-around go-to guy for keeping this place up and running. Ed, this is Jillian Jones. She's going to be getting married here."

Ed Warren was a tall man with a stocky frame and gray hair that was balding on top. Appearing to be roughly the same age as his wife, he had an open, welcoming face, which quickly eased into a smile. "Nice to meet you, ma'am."

"You, too," Jillian said. "You take care of this whole house? That's a big job for one man."

His smile deepened. "It keeps me busy," he

acknowledged before turning to his wife. "Rosie? There any coffee?"

"There should be half a pot," Rosie said with barely concealed irritation.

"There's not," Ed said patiently.

"Oh, for Pete's sake," Rosie said, shoving away from the table. "I know there was. And of course you can't make any more yourself."

"You know you don't like anybody messing around in your kitchen."

"That's because I know where everything goes," Rosie retorted. Without a glance back at Jillian and Meredith, she rounded the end of the table and followed her husband, who ducked back through the doorway before her.

The room immediately felt quieter when they were gone. "I'm sorry about that," Meredith said softly. "They can be a little…eccentric."

"It's fine," Jillian assured her. "They're part of the atmosphere of a place like this, an authentic staff of real people who are at home here, right?"

"I'm hoping people think so," Meredith admitted with a smile.

"So you kept on all the original staff?"

"We did. There were only four of them, though. Grace, Rosie, Ed and Ray, the grounds-keeper. Zack, who brought up your bags, is Ray's son. Jacob Sutton was apparently a recluse in his later years, and he pretty much kept a skeleton crew on staff. They've all been here for so long it didn't seem right to turn them out. Like you said, this is their home, and they've proven more than capable at their jobs. Of course we'll hire as much staff as necessary to work the wedding. I already have a long list of people from town on call."

"It sounds great. It's amazing that you're planning on doing so much with such a small regular staff, though."

"This is only for the time being. We may hire more people on a permanent basis. We're still evaluating how much more additional staff we'll need based on...how the future looks."

She glanced away, and Jillian understood her meaning. After what had happened to Courtney, the new wedding business wasn't on the strongest footing. The future would depend on what happened with the next wedding.

Which isn't going to happen, Jillian acknowledged with a trace of guilt.

She reminded herself she had no reason to feel guilty. As one of the owners, this woman was part of the cover-up of whatever had happened to Courtney, and might even be involved herself. Jillian couldn't forget that.

"So tell me about your fiancé," Meredith said brightly in a clear effort to change the subject. "I'd love to hear all about him."

It was a question Jillian was prepared for. "Ryan's an architect who works on projects all over the world. It's one reason he's as excited as I am to be married here. He's fascinated by Sutton Hall. He couldn't be more jealous that I get to see it first."

"Do you have a picture of him? I'd love to see what he looks like."

"Of course," Jillian said, reaching for her bag. She'd figured she'd be expected to have pictures of her fiancé and the two of them together. It would only make sense that a prospective bride would have plenty of them and be eager to show off her groom. Pulling out her wallet, she withdrew the plastic photo holder and handed it to Meredith, who began flipping through it.

"Oh, he's very handsome," Meredith said. Though it hardly mattered, Jillian knew she was being honest. By any reasonable standards, Ryan was a very good-looking man. He was also conveniently out of the country at the moment, so if anyone tried reaching him to confirm her story, they'd have a hard time doing so. It was a good thing, too, since she didn't want him finding out she was here any more than she wanted anyone here learning he wasn't her fiancé. Ryan would kill her if he knew she'd come here on her own and wouldn't hesitate to blow her cover.

Of course the downside of that was that no one

knew she was here. Just in case anything happened, she'd written an email to several people she trusted and set it to be sent on a time delay if she didn't reschedule it, which she planned to do every twenty-four hours. She also intended to add to the message with her thoughts and impressions of what she found here, letting them know about the investigation she was conducting and hopefully leaving relevant clues in case something did happen to her. With any luck, it wouldn't come to that.

"Everything all right in here?"

The voice came from the main entrance to the room—loud, startling...and familiar.

Adam Sutton.

It was all she could do not to tense as adrenaline suddenly ricocheted through her body. A strange reaction. She tried to tell herself it was because he'd startled her, even as part of her deep down recognized it was more than that.

He was behind her. It wasn't just that his voice had come from that direction. No, she immediately sensed his location, exactly where he was standing, mere feet away.

She recognized the feeling of that hard, steady gaze boring through her.

Then he was there, standing just behind them, positioned between her chair and Meredith's.

Keeping her expression carefully clear, she raised her head to look at him.

And met his eyes.

As she'd known he would, he was looking directly at her. A jolt went through her that she had to fight her hardest to keep from showing. It was exactly the reaction she hadn't had when she'd first seen Zack Hopkins.

It was also ridiculous. She didn't know this man. Everything about him said she shouldn't trust him, let alone feel…anything else toward him.

"Of course," Meredith said, finally answering his question. Her voice was tight—with nervousness? Something else? "Jillian was just showing me pictures of her fiancé."

"Really?" Adam said with a slight arch of his brow. "I'd love to see them."

Some kind of look Jillian couldn't read passed between brother and sister before Meredith thrust the photo holder at him.

Jillian watched as Adam slowly went through the photos, examining each one closely, eyes narrowed to slits. "What does your fiancé do?"

"He's an architect."

"Ah," he said in a tone that seemed to say he didn't believe her. "How did the two of you meet?"

"At a party," she said automatically. It was the

truth. "I'm afraid I don't have a more romantic story of our first meeting than that."

"All that matters is that you did meet," Meredith assured her.

When Adam reached the last photograph, he finally raised those dark eyes to her, an indecipherable look in them.

"You make a very attractive couple," he said blandly, reaching out to hand the photos back to her. "Congratulations."

"Thank you."

He continued to stare at her for a long moment before finally nodding, giving the table a cursory glance, a tight, unconvincing smile on his lips. "I'll let you ladies get back to business. Sorry to interrupt."

"Not a problem," Meredith said breezily, though again Jillian caught the look she shot him.

Curious, Jillian thought. There was so much going on beneath the surface she didn't know about around here. She had to wonder how much of it was relevant to her purposes. She was going to have to figure it out—and soon.

"Now then," Meredith said. "Why don't we talk about flowers?"

Jillian couldn't imagine anything she wanted to do less at the moment. Pasting on a smile, she made herself nod.

Keeping her attention on Meredith, Jillian turned away from Adam.

It didn't matter. She could still feel him there.

She sensed him begin to depart, relief piercing the tension gripping her insides.

Listening with half an ear to Meredith, she waited for the feeling to dissipate completely.

It didn't. Instead, fresh awareness prickled the back of her neck. And she knew.

He was watching her.

The tension holding her clenched tighter. A strange mix of emotions churned in her belly, twisting and changing into each other, making it hard to recognize them all. Wariness. Nervousness.

Excitement.

The last one made no sense, but she had no doubt it was the one that had her heart beating the hardest.

Even after he'd finally left, it took a while for the feeling to fade completely.

He was suspicious of her. She was convinced of that now. It was the only thing that made sense, the only possible reason for his unrelenting focus. There was none of Zack Hopkins's flirtatiousness in his intense scrutiny. Which was ironic considering the effect it seemed to be having on her.

She was going to have to be careful around

him. Or better yet, avoid him entirely. The man was a threat to her mission, and quite possibly, her life. She couldn't forget that.

No matter how many times she had to remind herself.

THIS ONE WAS different than the last. More reserved. Not as overly excited about the wedding plans and her upcoming nuptials.

Only time would tell just how different from the last one she truly was.

The last bride to come here, for all her excitement about the wedding preparations, hadn't been serious about what the commitment of her impending nuptials truly meant. At a time when she should have been thinking about nothing but her wedding and getting ready for married life, she'd been looking at a man who wasn't her fiancé in a way she had no business doing so when she was engaged to be married.

She hadn't been fit to be a bride, hadn't deserved all those wonderful plans she'd made. Not at all.

This new one would have to be watched as well.

Chapter Three

Jillian waited until two in the morning before making her move.

She'd taken a nap after dinner, partly because the exhaustion of traveling here and pretending to be something she wasn't, surrounded by people she didn't trust, had gotten to her, partly because there was nothing else for her to do. She needed everyone else in Sutton Hall to be in bed and out of her way, needed the place to herself so she could do what she had to.

She needed to see the tower bedroom, the one where Courtney had been staying.

The one with the balcony she'd fallen from.

The final few hours before Jillian thought it would be safe to proceed passed with agonizing slowness. She made notes of her first impressions of everyone she'd met since her arrival. She considered who might have wanted to hurt Courtney, and why.

She thought about Adam Sutton, with his

darkly handsome looks and solemn stares that seemed to see right through her, and pondered what exactly was lurking beneath that enigmatic face....

Finally it was time.

She hadn't heard a sound in hours. Hopefully that meant the rest of the household was tucked tightly in their beds.

Expecting to have to work in the dark of night, she'd packed a flashlight for this very moment. Moving to the door, she slowly eased it open and peered out into the darkness.

Silence lay heavily over Sutton Hall. At least over the part nearest to where she was. The place was so big a brass band could be playing in the other wing and she probably wouldn't hear it from here.

She couldn't see anything, either, the darkness as thick as the quiet. Gripping the flashlight tightly, she slipped into the hallway, carefully closing the door behind her.

She stood there, her back to it, and stared into the blackness, willing her eyes to adjust. She didn't want to turn on the flashlight just yet, in case anyone was nearby.

She knew where she was heading. She'd read the police report, studied maps of Sutton Hall. She knew where the tower bedroom was. Now it was just a matter of getting there.

The stairs to the next floor weren't far from her room. Finally, she was able to detect enough in the darkness to make her way there. She moved quickly on the balls of her feet, her steps silent on the plush carpet. Listening carefully for the slightest sound, she hurried up the stairs to the third floor.

Another vast, empty corridor completely devoid of lights, exactly like the one she'd just left, faced her. She took a few steps into the hallway, enough to be out of view from the stairs, and finally turned on the flashlight.

The thin beam created by the tool did little to calm her nerves. Somehow the house was more unsettling when viewed through that pale light than it had seemed in the dark. The beam didn't reach far, seeming to fade out only a few feet in front of her. Everything beyond it was hazy and instinct. It was an eerie feeling, as though anything could be lurking just out of its reach, or at its edges, hidden just out of view.

She turned left, her tension building the closer she came to her destination. She kept her mouth closed and breathed through her nose, trying to keep her breathing steady when her heart seemed to be pounding out of control. Every few steps, she glanced back, sending the beam of the flashlight shooting behind her, just in case anyone was there, sneaking up on her....

Then there it was. The corridor came to an abrupt end. Just before it was a final door on the right.

The door to the tower bedroom.

Focusing her light on the doorknob, she eased her way toward it.

When she was finally there, she reached a trembling hand out to grasp the knob. Taking a deep breath, she turned it.

It twisted easily, the latch giving way and releasing the door with a barely audible click.

Jillian froze, her body tensing in surprise. Frankly, she'd half expected it to be locked and thought she'd have to try to pick it. It would have made sense that they'd want to keep people from going into this room. Or maybe the Suttons had trusted that no one would come here.

Foolish of them.

Good for her.

Not about to waste any more time, she gently pushed the knob inward, moving slowly in case the hinges made any noise. She needn't have worried. The door swung open silently, gradually revealing the space within.

The room wasn't completely dark. Faint moonlight poured in from a long window on the far side of the space.

No, she realized, going still. Not a window. A door. Maybe a door to a balcony?

Swallowing hard, she stepped inside, easing the door shut behind her. Only when she heard the latch fasten did she reach over and fumble for the light switch on the wall. Her skin crawling at being in this room, with its long shadows and dark spaces, she struggled to find the switch, her heart beating faster each moment her fingers came away empty.

Her fingertips finally made contact. She instantly flipped the switch, flooding the room with blessed light.

Maybe too much? she wondered, imagining the light pouring out through the windows and into the night. Would it be visible from any of the other windows on one of the sides of the mansion that came together to form this tower?

Trying to visualize the layout of the house, she decided it was unlikely. Not to mention that, now that she was here, she didn't really feel like wandering around in the dark with only her flashlight to guide her. Not here. Not in this room.

Stepping forward, she surveyed the space. When she'd heard the room had had a balcony, she'd wondered why Courtney hadn't asked for another one given her fear of heights. Now that she was here, she could understand why. Jillian had thought the room she'd been put in had been impressive, but this one was magnificent, bigger and more extravagant, from the massive bed that could easily fit a half-dozen people to the stone fireplace on one wall that was practically the size of a full room itself. The space was warm and comfortable despite its size. The exit to the balcony was such a minor part of the room it would be easy enough to forget it was there at all.

Inevitably, though, Jillian's eyes found the doors, closed tightly against the night. She studied them from across the room, suddenly wary. This was it. A month ago Courtney had stood in this room, and then she'd found herself out there, and then—

"Looking for something?"

The voice came out of nowhere, shocking in the silence. Her heart leaping into her throat, she whirled around, automatically raising the flashlight to defend herself—

Adam Sutton stood just inside the door, arms folded over his chest, his expression as dark as the blackness that yawned beyond the open doorway.

She hadn't even heard the door open. The fact that he was standing there in that pose, obviously having been there for at least a few moments, told her he'd been watching her. And she wondered if he'd waited to speak until a moment that would startle her most.

That didn't mean she was going to be meek and defensive, even if she was somewhere she wasn't supposed to be. Slowly lowering the flashlight, she met his gaze head-on. "This is the room, isn't it? The one where the last bride stayed?"

"The one she fell to her death from?" he said, arching a brow. "I think you know full well that it is. The only real question is what you're doing here."

"You can't blame me for being curious."

"Can't I?" He stepped forward, arms dropping to his sides, moving toward her one slow step at a time, with the leonine grace of a predator gradually approaching its prey.

She didn't allow herself to take a step back, to retreat, to move at all. Even as her skin began to tingle the closer he came, with wariness, with unease…with something else that made her heart beat faster most of all.

He finally stopped a few feet away, not enough that he was really invading her space, but enough that he might as well have been. He towered over her, peering down into her eyes, the lines of his handsome face hard and cold. His presence was overwhelming, a palpable thing she felt too strongly. Her whole body seemed to buzz with awareness of it, of him. It was all she could do not to swallow hard.

Unsettled by the strange emotions churning inside her, she managed to hold her ground and found her voice. "If you wanted to keep people out, you should have locked the door."

"I did," he said, surprising her. "Right after the police were done with the room."

Jillian frowned, not understanding. "But it was unlocked."

He smiled, the slow curving of his lips sending a shiver of warning up her spine. "I unlocked it this evening and set a sensor to inform me if anyone opened the door. Just in case *someone* decided to come up here."

It couldn't have been clearer who that "someone" was. *A trap,* she thought. He'd set it specifically for her and she'd walked right into it. The only question was—

"Why? Why go to all that trouble?"

"Because I wanted to know just how much trouble you are."

"Indulging a little basic human curiosity is hardly causing trouble."

"If that's all you were doing," he said pointedly. "What are you really doing here, Ms. Jones?"

"I'm here to get married," she answered automatically.

"Are you?"

"If not, I've paid a very large deposit for no reason."

"Or for a different reason than the one you're claiming."

"And what would that be?"

He simply looked at her for a long moment, his eyes peering, unblinking, into hers. "You tell me."

"I have no idea. You seem to be the one with the active imagination. Maybe you should tell me what you want me to say."

He continued studying her with that cold, unwavering stare. With some effort, she managed to hold his gaze, refusing to back down or let the slightest weakness show.

His unyielding gaze slowly shifted, stroking over her face. Her skin burned wherever his eyes touched her, as they trailed over her nose, her cheeks, finally reaching her lips. She waited for them to move away. They didn't, lingering on her mouth, with an intensity of focus that sent a sudden rush of heat flooding through her.

Without warning, he abruptly turned away and stalked across the room.

Straight to the doors to the balcony.

Unease shooting through her, she watched as he grabbed the handles and pushed the doors open. Night wind blasted through the fresh gap between them, blowing through his hair and molding his clothes tightly against the hard lines of his body.

It took only seconds for the cold air to reach her. She barely noticed it, her attention fixed on the balcony. She couldn't really see it. The light flooding the room somehow didn't manage to reach far past the doors.

Staring at the endless emptiness beyond the open doors, she shivered, the reaction having nothing to do with the wind.

One thing she knew for sure, there was no way Courtney would have been out on that balcony at night.

Turning back to her, he gestured to the doors as though presenting the opening to her. "All right, Ms. Jones. You wanted to see it. Come take a look."

She remained where she was. He was right—it was what she'd come here for. But alone with this man, she suddenly didn't want to be anywhere near that balcony.

She turned her focus to him. He watched her through hooded eyes, the challenge clear in them.

"If I didn't know better, I'd think you were trying to scare me."

"I'm only giving you what you said you wanted. Or were you lying about that?"

"You know, for someone who's supposedly

running a business here, you're not exactly welcoming to paying customers. Aren't you worried I'll decide to leave?"

"No," he said flatly. "Because I don't think you will. I don't think there's anything I can say that could get you to leave."

"You're right, of course. If the idea of having my wedding in a place where another bride recently died doesn't scare me, I'm certainly not going to be scared off by you. But that's what you want, isn't it? For me to leave?"

"If you're lying about why you're here, then yes."

"Which you think I am. This is your property. If you want me to leave so badly, why don't you just kick me out?"

"Meredith wants you here. She believes you."

"It's nice to know paranoid fantasies don't run in the family."

Jillian wouldn't have thought it possible, but his expression actually darkened further. "This business means a great deal to my sister. I have no intention of letting her be hurt by someone who's here under false pretenses and wasting her time."

"Wouldn't it hurt her if I left? Another canceled wedding wouldn't be a good thing, even if the end result is less disturbing."

"It would be better than having her hurt by

you turning out to be something you're not. So let's have it, Ms. Jones. Who are you?"

A pang of guilt welled inside her, just for a moment, before she ruthlessly pushed it back down. Because while Meredith Sutton *might* be hurt, Courtney definitely had been, and she'd lost a great deal more than a business.

"Just a woman who wants to get married in a beautiful castle," she said simply, without blinking. "Isn't that every little girl's dream?"

A faint smile played across his lips. "So they say."

Suddenly she wanted nothing more than to get away. From this room, with its connection to Courtney's death. From that balcony, which seemed infinitely dangerous.

From this man, with his cool stare that left her feeling anything but cold.

She'd had enough of this game, and wasn't really up for fending off any more accusations—or dealing with the strange way he had of throwing her off-balance, in more ways than one.

Refusing to let him see her nerves, she squared her shoulders and held his gaze steadily. "I think I should be getting back to bed."

He simply stared at her with those bottomless, unreadable eyes. "Yes," he said coolly. "You should."

Raising her chin, she turned and headed for the exit.

She'd nearly reached the door and made her escape, relief beginning to swell in her chest, when he spoke again.

"Good night, Ms. Jones," he said in that faintly mocking tone. "Sleep tight."

She didn't bother looking back. She kept moving until she slipped through the open doorway, the sound of his voice sliding over her skin and nearly making her shudder, chasing her back into the darkness.

Chapter Four

After a few restless hours of tossing and turning, Jillian rose early. Her encounter with Adam Sutton had kept her up most of the night and plagued her dreams during the rest of it.

She couldn't get the image of his face out of her mind, couldn't stop trying to read whatever he'd been thinking behind that stony expression. Were his motives exactly as he'd said, nothing more than wanting to protect his sister and the business they were trying to build here from someone he thought was a liar? It was understandable, but was there more to it? Was there another reason he didn't want anyone poking around the circumstances of Courtney's death, because he knew it hadn't been an accident?

Worst of all, that wasn't the most disturbing part, or what kept her up most of the night.

Because when she'd been facing Adam Sutton's dangerous expression, both last night and in her dreams, the emotion that had her heart racing wildly hadn't been fear.

Not even close.

Irritated, she pushed the covers aside and climbed from the bed. His behavior made it clear she couldn't trust him. Even if he hadn't been threatening her, the man was still a threat to her mission here, a big obstacle keeping her from learning the truth about what happened to Courtney. Her reaction to the man made no sense. Not to mention it was disloyal to Courtney. She had no business feeling anything toward him as long as he was involved in this.

Showering and dressing quickly, she left the room in search of coffee. She didn't spot a single person as she made her way downstairs, passing through the cavernous front hall and into the expansive dining room. She only briefly hesitated before pushing through the swinging door into the kitchen. As she'd proven last night, as long as she was here she wasn't going to be averse to going places she maybe wasn't supposed to be. It might be the only way she was going to find anything out.

She just had to hope Adam Sutton wouldn't be lying in wait, she thought as a tremor quaked through her.

He wasn't. The only person in sight was Rosie, all alone in the massive room, bustling around behind the main counter. She didn't notice Jillian's entrance. Jillian opened her mouth to announce her presence, only to decide against it, taking advantage of the other woman's lack of awareness to study her.

Rosie kept in almost constant motion, checking whatever she had baking in the oven, tending to the meat frying on the stove, laying out her work on trays she had lined up on the counter. A slight smile played on her lips and she was humming as she worked, the very picture of contentment. She was clearly in her domain here and took obvious pleasure in her work. If Jillian hadn't already been hungry, the smells Rosie was creating would have changed that fast.

Rosie suddenly glanced up, her gaze colliding with Jillian's, eyes flaring wide in surprise.

"Oh!" she said, jolting upright. "I didn't see you there."

"I'm sorry," Jillian said, moving forward into the room. "I didn't mean to startle you."

The woman fluttered a hand as she started to turn back to the oven. "No harm, no foul. I was so busy with what I'm doing I probably wouldn't have noticed if an army came marching through here."

Jillian stepped up to the counter. "Whatever it is you're working on, it smells wonderful."

Rosie's smile deepened. "It's nice to have people in the house again to cook for. When Mr. Sutton—Mr. *Jacob* Sutton, that is—was still here, he didn't have guests too often, so there wasn't much reason to cook a large meal. It was just him and Grace, and me and Ed. Not much point cooking a big meal for four people. It's good to know I haven't forgotten how to do it."

"From the looks of things, you certainly haven't," Jillian said, eyeing the row of croissants Rosie had lying on a tray on the counter. "Where did you learn to cook like this?"

"Oh, my mother taught me. I asked her to when I was just a girl. I always dreamed of getting married and being a good wife. I know that's not fashionable to say these days, but it's true. I wanted a husband and children and to take care of my family. That was my dream."

"And then you met Ed."

Rosie's smile tightened, the enthusiasm noticeably dimming from her expression. "Yes. Ed."

Curious about the woman's reaction to the mention of her husband, Jillian studied her closely. "Do you have children?"

"I'm afraid not," Rosie said, a wistful note in her voice. "It wasn't meant to be."

"I'm sorry."

"It's all right. We don't always get what we want. Sometimes we have to make do with what we have."

"At least you still get to share your gifts," Jillian pointed out.

The woman instantly brightened. "That's true."

"You must have been excited when Adam and Meredith decided to open Sutton Hall for weddings."

"Oh, of course. Who doesn't love a wedding?"

"Did you get to work much with the last bride who came here?"

Rosie's expression didn't change, but Jillian didn't miss the beat of hesitation before she answered. "A little bit."

"What was she like?" Jillian asked.

There was another slight pause before Rosie said, "She was very excited about her wedding." She quickly turned away toward the stove, putting her back to Jillian.

It was a vague answer that didn't reveal anything about Rosie's true thoughts about Courtney. Though she was doing her best to cover it, Rosie clearly wasn't comfortable with the subject. It was understandable given what had happened, but Jillian was too skeptical not to wonder if there was more to the woman's reticence.

Before she could press the woman further, a door leading outside suddenly opened. Moments later, Ed stepped into the room. He came to an abrupt stop as soon as he saw them, his eyes shifting between Jillian and Rosie in surprise.

"Morning," he said.

"Good morning," Jillian returned.

"Well, don't just stand there with the door open," Rosie said sharply. "Come in already, would you?"

"That's what I'm doing," Ed said patiently. He stepped over the threshold and closed the door behind himself. "You don't have to tear my head off."

"I wouldn't have to if you'd act like a civilized person."

"You don't need to tell me how to act."

"It seems to me that I do."

Jillian listened to the exchange with growing discomfort. Every word that came out of Rosie's mouth was harsh and cutting. Ed didn't even fight back, his tone easygoing, his smile never wavering.

Then Rosie turned around and Jillian caught a glimpse of the look that entered Ed's eyes as he stared at his wife's back. The hardness, the utter coldness in his stare as he watched her, shocked Jillian to the core, sending a tremor of unease through her. Evidently the man wasn't nearly as indifferent to his wife's barbs as he seemed.

His gaze suddenly shifted to Jillian. As soon

as he saw she was looking at him, he quickly lowered his eyes to the table.

Eager to lighten the tension that had built in the room, Jillian interjected, "Rosie was just telling me how her mother taught her how to cook."

Ed raised his eyes back to her face. "You might want to be careful. Rosie'll talk your ear off if you let her."

The words were light, his easy smile firmly in place. But the look in his eyes was dead serious, as though the warning was more than a simple joke and one she should heed.

Jillian wasn't sure what the undercurrents between the couple meant. She only knew the room suddenly felt unbearably claustrophobic with all the tension—unspoken and otherwise—in the room.

"You know, I think I could use some fresh air," Jillian said, pushing to her feet. "I'll see you later."

Rosie quickly turned from the stove. "Breakfast is almost ready," she said sternly.

"I usually don't eat much in the morning," Jillian lied. "I'll grab something later." Ignoring Rosie's disapproving frown, Jillian gave her a little wave and pushed through the swinging door into the dining room before the cook could say anything.

Almost as soon as the door was at her back,

Jillian relaxed slightly, some of the tension instantly easing from her shoulders.

She was midway through the foyer when she heard the clack of heels on the marble floors approaching from the other side. Bracing herself, she watched as Grace stepped into the space moments later.

The woman instantly spotted her, acknowledging her with a nod. "Good morning, Ms. Jones."

"Morning, Grace. And please, it's Jillian, remember?"

"Very well," Grace said with just as much formalness.

"I thought I'd go out and explore the grounds a bit, try to get a feel for the property."

The corners of the woman's mouth turned down slightly. "Perhaps you should wait for Ms. Sutton to come down, or Mr. Sutton."

"That won't be necessary," Jillian said breezily, never hesitating on her way to the door. "I'm sure I can find my way around."

Jillian fully expected the woman to object further, but Grace didn't say another word. Moments later, Jillian pushed through the door and stepped outside.

A sigh automatically eased from her lungs. Stopping on the front stoop, she tilted her head back and closed her eyes, breathing in the fresh air. It was a beautiful spring day, crisp and clear, the sun warm on her face. More important, after nearly a day inside Sutton Hall, it felt good to be out in the open again. No, more than that, it was a relief not to be surrounded by stone walls, no matter how spacious the areas between them.

Finally opening her eyes, she turned left, once again knowing where she was heading from her study of the property maps. The gardens were on the east side of the building.

It took her only a few minutes to reach them, an explosion of greenery bursting with spring meeting her eyes. She could tell immediately the gardens were vast, the greenery extending far beyond what she could see.

An arched gable marked the entrance to them. Jillian stopped in front of it but didn't step inside. The gardens weren't what she was interested in.

Turning, she looked down along the side of the mansion to the rear, and what wasn't visible from the front.

And there it was.

The tower balcony.

Her heart jumped, seemingly as high as the balcony itself. It looked so insubstantial from this vantage point, a mere speck barely clinging to the wall, as though a mere breeze could sweep it from the building.

No, she thought, the certainty hardening in her gut and inspiring fresh anger. There was no way Courtney would have been out there. Just the idea of it was almost as inconceivable as the thought of her...

Plummeting from it.

"Well, hello there."

Jillian recognized the low, insinuating voice behind her before she saw the speaker. The wheedling tone had her skin crawling, but Jillian didn't let it show on her expression, bracing herself as she turned to face him.

As expected, Zack Hopkins stood a few feet away, leaning on the handle of a shovel he balanced between his hands. His gaze raked over her leisurely from head to toe, sending her skin crawling.

"Good morning," she said politely.

"You're up early," he noted.

"Yes, well, there's a lot to do. I wanted to get a chance to look around a bit, become more familiar with the grounds."

"I'd be happy to show you around, if you like."

"That's all right. I don't want to take you away from your work."

"Eh, it's nothing that can't wait. I think I'd have a lot more fun keeping you company."

The innuendo was more than clear, and she almost shook her head. "Are you flirting with me?" she asked, unable to hide her disbelief.

"Can you blame me?"

"I think I can. You do know I'm engaged to be married."

Shrugging one shoulder carelessly, he gave her what she suspected was intended to be a devastating grin. Which it still sort of was, she had to admit in spite of everything. Too bad the guy's overall sleaze factor severely outweighed his charm. "That means you're not married yet."

"I still made a commitment. You don't have any respect for that?"

His grin turned sardonic. "Commitments mean different things to different people. Some women don't take them as seriously as others."

Suspicion prickled the back of her neck. "Are you speaking from experience?"

"Seems to fit most women I've met."

"What about your mother?"

His expression hardened slightly. "My mother took off when I was a kid."

"I'm sorry. That must have been hard for you."

He shrugged again, the gesture seeming a little forced. "It is what it is. No reason for her to stick around if she didn't want to. Maybe she had the right idea. Take things too seriously, it'll drive you crazy. I mean, look at Old Man Sutton."

All of Jillian's instincts instantly went on alert. "What about him?"

Grimacing, Zack brushed off the comment with a wave of his hand. "Nothing," he muttered.

"Zack!" a male voice suddenly rang out sharply, causing the young man to stiffen.

Jillian looked past him to see an older man walking toward them. In his late fifties or early sixties, he was tall and broad-shouldered, with brown hair streaked with gray. His face was heavily lined with age and what she suspected were many years of working in the sun. His features settled into a heavy frown.

"Don't you have work you should be doing?" the man said before he reached them.

"Yes, Dad," Zack said. His posture tight with resentment, he turned away from Jillian without another word, skulking off into the gardens.

Jillian turned her attention to the newcomer. "You must be Ray," she said, remembering what Meredith had told her yesterday. "I'm Jillian."

"I know who you are," he said, his tone conveying he wasn't overly impressed with that knowledge. "I'm sorry if he was bothering you."

"Not at all," Jillian said diplomatically. "He was just being...friendly."

The man grunted. "Yeah, he's real good at being *friendly.* I'll make sure he stays out of your way."

"It must be nice having your son working with

you," she said quickly when he started to turn away, not wanting to lose him just yet.

"It's a good way to keep an eye on him," Ray said.

"Does he need someone to keep an eye on him?" she asked curiously.

He gave her a head-to-toe once-over, as his son had, but there was no interest in his gaze. "Most people do," he said vaguely.

"What about Mr. Sutton, the previous owner?"

"What do you mean?"

"Zack was telling me a little about him. Made it sound like he might have gone a little…crazy?"

The man's mouth tightened into a hard, unyielding line. "The boy talks too much."

Before she could say another word, he put his back to her and stalked into the gardens, quickly vanishing behind the hedge.

She could chase after him and ask him to show her the gardens in hopes of drawing out the conversation, but somehow she doubted running after him like that was going to make him any more talkative. She was going to have to find another approach to get him to open up to her, even a little, if that was even possible.

Instead, she drew in a deep breath of the warm morning air, tilting her head back to feel the sun on her face again. It was still bright out, the sky clear and blue, but Jillian suddenly felt inexplicably colder.

She needed answers, and if no one at Sutton Hall was willing to tell her what she needed to know, she'd have to go outside to get them.

And as she glanced up at the balcony hanging far in the sky, getting away from Sutton Hall for a little while didn't seem like such a bad idea.

Chapter Five

"We need to talk about Jillian Jones."

After waiting for hours to speak with Meredith, Adam didn't wait for her to close the office door behind her before launching into the topic.

Meredith shot him an exasperated look. "What is it now?"

"I caught her in the tower bedroom last night. The one Courtney Miller was staying in."

The clarification wasn't necessary, Meredith's gaze dimming before he offered it. She knew full well where Courtney Miller had been staying. She was the one who'd put her there, a fact he knew she still felt guilty about, though it certainly wasn't her fault the woman hadn't had enough sense not to venture out onto a balcony in a fierce wind and tumble off of it.

"I thought it was locked," she murmured.

Adam swallowed a twinge of guilt. "I must have forgotten to lock it the last time I went to check that everything was cleared out."

Meredith's eyes narrowed with suspicion, and he knew exactly what she was thinking. He never "forgot" to do things. It was something he took a great deal of pride in.

She evidently decided to let the issue pass. "What was she doing there?" she asked.

"Nosing around. Said she was curious."

"Well, you can hardly blame her for that. Honestly, I think it would be more suspicious if she wasn't."

It was exactly what Jillian Jones had said, Adam remembered with no small irritation. And both she and his sister were right. The fact that Jillian claimed not to care that another bride had recently died in the place she herself intended to be married had struck him as suspicious. If anything, the revelation that she wasn't quite so indifferent to that information should serve as a relief of some kind.

Instead, their encounter had only left him more wary of the woman than ever. The fact that she'd had a flashlight meant she'd specifically intended to snoop around when she came here. There was no other reason for her to bring one, or simply happen to have one in her luggage. And when he'd confronted her, she hadn't been at all embarrassed or remorseful at having been caught in the middle of the night somewhere she had no right to be. She hadn't backed down in the least, dodging every accusation and doing her best to turn the tables on him. She was smart, she was a fighter and she was determined.

Under different circumstances he might have respected that. She was a worthy adversary.

At the moment, an adversary was the last thing he needed, especially a worthy one. She wasn't going to be scared off easily.

The image of how she'd looked rose in his mind. Shoulders squared, spine straight, her green eyes flashing fire as she'd faced him.

A far different spark in those eyes, her supple mouth pursed gently, as she peered up at him, mere inches away…

She'd been dressed for bed, in a thin white T-shirt and loose cotton pants that clung to her hips. She should have looked small, vulnerable. She hadn't. Even with the wind filling the room, blowing the clothes against her body so that every curve, every tempting swell, was clearly outlined, she'd looked strong. Determined.

Tempting as hell.

"What is this really about?"

Adam jerked his head up, the words snapping him out of his thoughts. "What do you mean?"

Meredith folded her arms over her chest. "Jillian's been here less than twenty-four hours and I haven't heard you talk about anything else since she arrived."

"Because I don't trust her."

"Is that really what it is?"

"What are you suggesting?" he said, already suspecting he knew, unease crawling up the nape of his neck.

"She's a very attractive woman."

Meredith didn't have to elaborate. He had no trouble picking up on the implication. Maybe because the same notion had been percolating in the back of his mind, bubbling just beneath the surface.

"You're imagining things."

"Am I? It's been years since I've heard you talk this much about any woman. In fact, I don't actually remember you *ever* talking this much about a woman."

That was because he hadn't, Adam acknowledged reluctantly. He'd always been so consumed with work he'd never had time for anything serious, and never met a woman who'd made him want to change that.

"She's getting married," he said, unable to keep the hint of irony from his tone.

"You seem to have your doubts about that," Meredith pointed out. "Or is it because you don't want her to be?"

"No, because that would make her a liar and a fraud, and we'd have a much bigger problem on our hands."

"Actually, I think that would be less of a problem than you being interested in a woman who's very much attached and who came here to get married."

"Trust me, my only interest in her is why she's really here."

Even as he said it, he knew it was a lie.

If he was right, then he was attracted to a woman who was a liar, and probably worse. If he wasn't, then he was attracted to a woman who was completely off-limits. He wasn't going to chase after a woman who was marrying someone else.

Either way, he had no business thinking about her at all.

From the look on her face, Meredith didn't believe him any more than he did. He waited for her to call him on it, but she didn't.

"Good. Then we don't have a problem."

"Unless she gives us one."

"It's fine," she said firmly. "Everything is going to be fine."

Adam almost wondered how she could be capable of such optimism and hope after everything she'd been through.

The words were definitive, but Adam caught the barely noticeable tremor in her voice, the slightly tremulous quality of the smile she worked up. He knew her too well. He knew deep down she was trying to convince herself as much as she was him, as though if she tried hard enough, she could will it to be true. Because she wanted everything to work out, needed it to for reasons he understood all too well.

He would give anything to make it true.

But every instinct told him he couldn't, any more than he had in the past. At least this time he could keep her from getting hurt.

Even as part of him wondered if there was any chance he would be more successful at that than he'd been before.

UNABLE TO SHRUG off her wedding-planning duties any earlier without it looking suspicious, Jillian waited until lunch to announce she intended to drive into town, saying she wanted to explore the area a bit.

"I can come with you," Meredith offered. "I could show you some spots you might want to know about so you can point them out to your wedding guests as places to visit."

"That's all right," Jillian said. "I think I'd like to try to get a feel for the area on my own."

"Of course," Meredith said, forcing a smile. Jillian didn't miss the worry the woman could barely conceal. Was she concerned Jillian wouldn't come back? Jillian wondered if Meredith was aware her brother was trying to scare her off, or if she had other reasons to be worried. It was just another of the mysteries at Sutton Hall, and Jillian already had enough of those to unravel.

She left midafternoon, finding her way to the garage where her rental car had been parked. The tension tightening the back of her shoulders eased slightly as she drove away. She glanced back in the rearview mirror once. The mansion completely filled the reflective surface, looming as large as ever. It didn't look as dark and gloomy as it did up close, but Jillian still felt unsettled as she took it in. Only when the trees blocked it did the mansion finally disappear from view. The instant it did, an involuntary sigh eased from Jillian's lungs. Inhaling deeply, she turned her focus to the road.

The town of Hawthorne was located a few miles down the road at the base of the mountain. Jillian hadn't paid much attention to it on her way through the day before, too intent on reaching her destination. This time she made a point to study her surroundings as she entered the town limits. It was even smaller than she'd realized, but utterly charming, with a comfortable small-town feel. The buildings that lined the main street were large and older, classic in style. She wouldn't have been surprised to learn they'd all been standing for more than a century, all beautifully maintained.

Spotting the library, Jillian parked out front and made her way inside. The building was quiet as she entered, even more than she would have expected for a library. The only person in view was the woman behind the front desk. Appearing to be in her fifties, with a head of brown curls and half-rimmed glasses, she looked up and smiled at Jillian's approach.

"Hi there," Jillian said. "I'm hoping you can help me. I'm interested in doing some research on Sutton Hall."

The woman's expression didn't change, but Jillian didn't miss the way her smile seemed to tighten slightly. "What kind of research?"

"My name is Jillian Jones. I'm going to be getting married there and would love to learn more about the place. The new owners have told me a little, but I'm sure there's more they don't know about since they're fairly new to the place themselves. I thought I might try to do some research on my own."

With every word, the woman's smile had tightened further. By the time Jillian finished her explanation, it couldn't have looked more forced. "How nice," the woman said faintly. "You must be so excited. Are your friends and family up there with you preparing for the big day?"

"No, it's just me at the moment."

The woman's eyebrows lifted. "Oh, so you're... all alone out there."

The way she said it sent a shiver down Jillian's spine, reminding her all too well how true it was. "Well, not exactly," she made herself say. "The Suttons and the rest of the staff are there, too, of course."

"Of course," the woman echoed flatly.

"I know what you're thinking," Jillian said. "And yes, I am aware of the death that happened there recently, so you don't have to tell me about that."

The look on the woman's face said she clearly needed to if Jillian was dismissing it that easily.

As if realizing she hadn't said anything for far too long, the woman straightened with a start. "All right," she said finally. She motioned toward a nearby table. "Why don't we have a seat and I'll tell you what I can."

"That sounds great," Jillian replied, not having to fake her eagerness. She'd thought the woman might point her to some reference materials, but this was better. Especially since some of the things she wanted to know were unlikely to be in any books.

With a nod, Jillian moved toward the table, glancing around the room as she made her way there. There didn't seem to be any other patrons at the moment, luckily enough for her since it gave the woman time to talk.

The librarian followed Jillian to the table, taking the seat across from her with a clear view to keep an eye on the door. "I'm Emma, by the way," she said, introducing herself.

"I'm glad to meet you," Jillian said honestly. "The folks at Sutton Hall haven't been all that talkative."

"I'm not surprised," Emma confessed. "The folks up there have always kept to themselves. Has to be odd for them to have strangers around."

"I can understand that. But I'm still fascinated by the place and would love to find out everything I can about it."

The librarian pursed her lips, considering. "All right. Well, let's see…Sutton Hall was built in 1874 by Hugh Sutton, a manufacturing tycoon who owned a number of factories throughout New England. Jacob Sutton, the last owner before the current ones, was Hugh's great-grandson. He was an only child, and he and his wife never had children, which is why the place was inherited by Adam and Meredith, who are descendants of one of Hugh's other sons."

"I heard Jacob's wife died in a car accident," Jillian said.

"That's right. About twenty-five years ago. It was during a winter storm. Her car went right off the road and over the edge of the mountain. It took some time to reach the car and get her body out. Jacob blamed himself. They were supposed to be traveling together. He should have been in the car with her."

"Did he think he could have done a better job driving in the storm?"

"Or he thought he could have died with her. It often seemed like he wished he had. The way he lived the rest of his life, I'm not sure he didn't."

"What do you mean?"

"He never really left Sutton Hall after that. He sold off most of his business interests. As far as I know, he didn't work. He didn't have to, of course. Between his investments and the family fortune, I'm sure he had more than enough to live on for far longer than he did."

Jillian had already thought Jacob Sutton's story was sad, but the more she heard about him the more tragic it seemed. "Rosie mentioned that he seldom had guests. I guess I didn't realize just how reclusive he'd become."

"He hadn't been seen in town in more than twenty years, though a few people who went up to the house for various reasons saw him. They said he was practically wasting away, a shadow of the man he'd once been. I don't think anyone was surprised to hear he'd died."

"I heard he might have gone a little...crazy in his last few years?"

The woman's eyes narrowed shrewdly. "I'm guessing you heard that from Zack."

"How'd you know?"

Emma grimaced. "If anyone was liable to tell you that, it's him. The rest of them up there are all too loyal, and Zack likes to talk. Most of what I've heard about Jacob in the last years of his life started with Zack talking here in town and word getting around. But, yes, from what I hear Jacob spent most of his days sitting on the balcony of one of the tower rooms, the one that looks out over the road leading up the mountain. He'd just sit there and stare, as if he was still watching for her, waiting for her to come back."

The balcony of the tower room that looks out over the road leading up the mountain. Jillian didn't need her to tell her which one that was, as a prickle of unease raised goose bumps on her arms. It was the one with the best view in the house.

The one that Courtney had fallen from...

No wonder Zack hadn't wanted to tell her about it.

"He must have really loved her," Jillian managed to say.

Emma smiled sadly. "I'd say so. A few years after Kathleen died, someone in town asked him if he'd considered finding a new wife. He said, 'A Sutton man loves forever.' I guess that's true. All the Sutton men going back to old Hugh were only married once and stayed married to their wives until one of them passed away."

A Sutton man loves forever. Jillian wondered idly if that was really true for all Sutton men, including the one currently living there....

As soon as she realized where her thoughts were going, she put a quick end to them. Adam Sutton's romantic loyalty hardly mattered, and certainly wasn't something she had any reason to be interested in.

"Did you know her?" Jillian asked, more curious than ever about the woman she knew only as the bride in the portrait at Sutton Hall, a woman capable of inspiring such devotion. "Kathleen Sutton?"

"Not personally. I saw her in town a few times. I remember she was very beautiful. And everyone seemed to think well of her. Practically the whole town mourned when she died."

All of this was interesting, but it wasn't getting Jillian to what she really needed to know: what had happened to Courtney, and who might be responsible.

"What about the staff?" Jillian asked. "Meredith said she and her brother kept on all of the people who'd been working there when Jacob

Sutton died. I guess it was just the four of them—Grace, Rosie, Ed and Ray?"

"That's true. That was nice of them to do that. They didn't have to, and I'm sure they could have found younger people to handle the more strenuous jobs, especially Ed and Ray's. But those four have been there so long, I'm not sure where any of them would have gone."

Jillian could sense the woman being diplomatic, her words carefully couched, a wealth of unspoken thought behind them. "You don't like them," Jillian challenged to get her to cut to the chase.

Emma's eyes widened in surprise, but Jillian didn't miss how she didn't exactly rush to deny it. "I wouldn't say that," she said slowly. "I can't say I really know them. No one does. I mean, to live and work out there all these years, in such an isolated place. I suppose it takes an…unusual kind of person to do that. People thought Jacob was odd for becoming a recluse. But the truth is, none of the rest of them is all that different. They all keep to themselves out there just as much."

The woman's comments only confirmed Jillian's own impressions of the Sutton Hall staff. "What *can* you tell me about them?"

"Well, there's Grace, of course. Before the new owners arrived, she was pretty much in charge of the place. Even when Jacob was alive, anyone who had any business out there got the sense she was the real boss. He basically left her to run it as she saw fit."

"I'm guessing she wasn't too happy to have a couple of strangers inherit and take over Sutton Hall."

"I can't imagine she was, not that I've ever heard her say anything. Grace has never been overly chatty. Or maybe there's nobody in town she figures is worth her time to talk to," she added under her breath.

"She doesn't have any friends or family nearby?"

"Not that I know of. Grace isn't originally from the area. I'm not sure where she's from actually. She came to Sutton Hall with Kathleen when she married Jacob. I think she must have worked for Kathleen before. She was just a maid then. After Kathleen died and most of the staff left for whatever reason, Grace gradually seemed to take charge, until she was running the place."

Jillian tried to picture Grace as a fresh-faced young woman arriving at Sutton Hall as a mere maid. She couldn't manage it. Every trace of that young woman seemed long gone, leaving a woman who gave every appearance of being as much an institution as the place itself. "And she's been there all this time? Never married or had a family of her own?"

"No. She's been there for thirty years. I've never heard talk of her seeing anybody or anything. She just stayed out there."

"What about Ed and Rosie?"

"They aren't from around here, either. They showed up about twenty-five years ago when Jacob was looking for a new cook. Rosie interviewed for the job, and Ed managed to talk his way into getting hired as a caretaker, which was sorely needed. From the sound of it, Ed was the only one keeping the place standing. He must have done a great job of it. After they took over, the younger Suttons hired some people to work on renovating and restoring the place, and it didn't take them long, only a few months. From what I heard, there wasn't that much work that needed doing, much less than anyone would have thought, which has to be one reason the Suttons kept Ed on, as well as Rosie to cook."

"Their marriage doesn't seem all that happy."

Emma shrugged. "I wouldn't know much about that. Like I said, they tend to keep to themselves up there at the house. Neither of them became all that friendly with anyone in town, even after all these years."

"What about Ray? Zack said his mother left them?"

"That's right. Zack was just a boy then, maybe three or four. Carolyn took off one day. Ray said she left a note saying she wanted something else from her life and was leaving to find it, and that was that. I can't say I was surprised. Just about everyone knew Carolyn didn't like living out there. Not many could blame her for that. It's so secluded out there, and I'm sure it had to be lonely, especially during the winter whenever they got snowed in, with only Ray and Zack to talk to, and maybe Rosie. Can't imagine her and Grace being all that close. Those two were complete opposites."

"She didn't try to take Zack?"

"Carolyn…wasn't really the mothering type." Emma lowered her voice. "Truth be told, the main reason she and Ray got married was because she was pregnant, and there was talk about whether Ray was really Zack's father."

"Did they ever hear from her again?"

"Not that I ever heard. She never returned to the area, and word never got back about where she ended up."

Jillian could understand why Zack was so jaded. Not only had the woman walked away from her commitment to her marriage, her duty as a mother apparently hadn't meant much to her, either. It wasn't surprising he might have issues with women. Ray, too, for that matter.

"Ray never remarried?" she asked.

"No. I can't think of him seeing anyone after

Carolyn was gone. He just raised Zack and kept working up there, about near becoming as reclusive as the rest of them."

"I get the feeling Zack thinks he's quite the ladies' man."

Emma smiled wryly. "I think it's the young ladies in the area who give him that impression. I'm sure you've noticed he's quite handsome. From what I can tell, he's been able to have his pick of female company, and he's taken full advantage of that. A real love-'em-and-leave-'em type. I guess he's more like his mother than his father in that regard. And he's always been talking about leaving the area, so I guess there's that, too. He actually did move to Boston last year, but he came back a few months ago."

That seemed strange, since he didn't seem all that enthused about working at Sutton Hall. "Why did he come back?"

"Nobody knows. As much as he likes to talk, he's been real tight-lipped about that. Guess it didn't work out for him in the city."

This was exactly the kind of stuff Jillian had hoped to learn, inside information on the people at Sutton Hall that might help her better understand who they were and what made them tick. It had also come a lot easier than she'd expected.

Jillian surveyed the librarian carefully, trying to get more of a sense of who she was exactly.

Her tone wasn't exactly gossipy, more matter-of-fact than anything, but she certainly wasn't sparing many details. "I appreciate the information, but I have to admit, I'm a little surprised you're sharing so much about these people's private lives with a complete stranger."

Emma lowered her eyes briefly. "If you're going to be married there, I suppose it's only fair you know about the people up there."

Jillian frowned, suspicion nudging at the back of her mind. Most people wouldn't think it was necessary to learn about the personal lives of the staff handling a wedding. Unless… "I saw your reaction when I told you I was getting married there. Be honest with me. Do you think there's some reason I shouldn't?"

"I wouldn't say that…."

Jillian bit back her impatience, wishing the woman would just spit out what she *would* say. "Tell me, what do you think happened to the woman who died there?"

Emma hesitated, the pause so noticeable it was almost answer enough. "They said it was an accident," she said carefully.

"But what do *you* think?" Jillian pressed.

Emma slowly licked her lips, not quite meeting Jillian's eyes. "It's just…my husband always said that to live out there, all isolated like that, it's almost like the folks out there were hiding from the world. And you have to wonder exactly why it is they're hiding.... And the idea of that woman just *falling* from a balcony... It's kind of hard to imagine."

Yes, it is, Jillian thought, anger stirring in her gut.

"On the other hand, it was a windy night," Emma conceded. "Being that high up, she could have gotten too close, maybe gotten disoriented. Maybe it *was* an accident. Without any proof otherwise, the police couldn't say it wasn't. I really can't, either."

I can, Jillian thought, more certain than ever.

Perhaps misreading Jillian's expression, Emma leaned forward and met her eyes. "I'm not trying to scare you off, believe me. It would be good for the town if the Suttons were able to get this wedding business going. They've talked about hiring part-time workers as needed and people around here could use those jobs, and it would generate a lot of revenue for local businesses. Which is just more reason why I don't want anything to happen to you."

"But you think there's enough of a chance of that happening that you wanted to warn me?"

"No..." Emma shook her head. "I'm probably just being foolish. Look, I hope your wedding goes perfectly and is everything you dream of. But there's always been something a little strange about that place and the folks up there. So it couldn't hurt to be careful. Watch out for yourself. Just in case…"

IT WAS GETTING dark when Jillian finally left the library. She continued to turn Emma's words over in her mind as she started the drive back to Sutton Hall.

Knowing that even one person thought there was something suspicious about Courtney's death, someone who didn't have a personal stake in it, gave her fresh confidence that she wasn't wrong. Something had happened to Courtney, something that may have been done to her by one of the people at Sutton Hall.

You have to wonder exactly why it is they're hiding….

Emma's words could have been nothing more than small-town suspicions of outsiders, people who chose to live separate from the rest. And maybe that was part of it. Except Jillian had already been wondering what secrets the Sutton Hall staff were hiding even before she'd spoken to the woman.

And it wasn't just the staff. It was the Suttons themselves. Emma knew even less about them, but they were mysteries just as much as the people who worked for them. Meredith Sutton, with her nervousness and skittish eyes.

Adam Sutton, with his dark warnings and cool aloofness.

A mystery she had to solve, even as the thought of the man sent a little tremor through her.

She'd just turned onto the winding road leading up the mountain to Sutton Hall when the engine began to sputter. Frowning, she glanced down in confusion at the instrument panel. The light illuminating it began to flicker, the gauges starting to waver, then dip ominously. She didn't even have time to consider steering the car onto the side of the road before it came to a complete stop.

She sat there in confusion for a few moments, not understanding what had just happened. With numb fingers, she reached out, turned off the ignition, then tried to start it again.

The engine chugged, groaned and refused to turn over.

A few more tries only yielded the same result. The car wasn't going anywhere.

It had been running fine on the way into town, not to mention on the long drive from the airport yesterday. Suspicion sparked in the back of her mind. Was it possible someone had tampered with it? But for what reason?

Maybe to do exactly what had happened and

strand her alone in the middle of nowhere, she thought with a flicker of unease. She stared at the long, dark road before her, then back toward the stretch she'd just come down. She couldn't see anything up ahead in either direction but trees and road. Darkness was falling quickly, long shadows already stretching across the pavement. It wouldn't be long before it was completely black out here.

Suppressing a shudder, she pulled out her cell phone and checked for a signal.

Nothing.

Of course. She grimaced. She was out in the country, on a mountain of all things. Cell phone coverage was probably the last thing she should be counting on.

Grabbing her bag, she climbed out of the car. Raising the phone in front of her, she turned in a slow circle, trying to get even a hint of a signal. After turning around several times and failing to summon a single bar, she had to concede it wasn't going to happen.

Lowering the phone, Jillian glanced in either direction again, trying to gauge whether she was closer to town or Sutton Hall at this point. Either way, it seemed unlikely she could count on anyone happening by anytime soon. In the meantime, the road somehow seemed even darker than it had been moments before, the pavement barely visible, the night closing in around her.

Naturally she'd left her flashlight back in her room, never thinking she'd need it.

She wondered how long it would be before anyone came looking for her.

If they came looking for her.

Either way, she couldn't stand there forever. There was probably more of a chance she'd encounter a vehicle on the main road than on the one to Sutton Hall. She'd be better off heading back into town and hoping someone passed by.

She was about to start in that direction when lights suddenly swept over her, followed quickly by the sound of an approaching engine. Foreboding prickling the skin at the nape of her neck, she glanced up.

It looked like a car, coming up on the road. She could barely make out its details in the darkness.

She wondered if the driver saw her, if she needed to flag his or her attention....

Or if she even wanted to, she suddenly thought with a trace of nervousness. Maybe it was no coincidence the car had appeared on this lonely stretch of road so soon after hers broke down. Whoever it was, the driver had her all alone out here....

Before she could shake her doubts and decide what to do, the car began to slow as it approached. The driver had clearly spotted her. Or been looking for her, knowing she was likely to be here?

She had no weapon, no way to defend herself—

The car came to a stop beside her. The window slowly rolled down, and even before she bent to peer inside she knew who she'd see.

Adam Sutton looked back at her, one eyebrow raised, his face shadowed in darkness, lit only by the console in front of him. "Problem?"

Don't you already know? she nearly asked, biting back the words. Whether or not he was responsible, this probably wasn't the best time to tick him off, not when she was alone and defenseless on the side of the road.

"My car broke down. I'm not sure what's wrong with it."

If he was surprised, he didn't acknowledge it. He simply nodded. "Come on," he said with a tip of his head. "I'll give you a ride back. You can call the rental company to come check it out."

She hesitated just the slightest moment, her suspicions lingering a little too long, asking whether she really wanted to get in that car with him....

But the offer was entirely reasonable, of course. And if he wanted to do something to her, he could have done it here, where he had her alone, under the guise of helping her with the car.

She reached for the door handle, her gaze meeting his.

She saw from the steady frankness in his eyes that he hadn't missed her pause. He didn't comment on it, but simply waited.

She wished she could read what lay in those cold black depths.

He didn't even smile, or try to offer her some reassuring gesture. He simply sat there, waiting.

Doing her best to shake the feeling she was willingly stepping into a trap, she pulled the door open and climbed inside.

Chapter Six

They rode in silence for a few minutes, the quiet lying thick and heavy between them. Adam did his best to keep his eyes on the road and off the maddening woman beside him.

Of course her car would have to break down just before he came along—if that was what had even happened. For all he knew he'd simply caught her when she was up to something out there and she'd used the breakdown as an excuse. He wouldn't put it past her.

Swallowing a sigh, he grimaced. Damn. The woman had him so turned around he barely knew which way was up.

Jillian cleared her throat gently, an obvious prelude to speaking, and he braced himself. "I didn't know you'd gone into town," she said mildly, though he thought he almost detected a hint of accusation in the words.

"No reason you should. I left after you did."

"What took you into town?"

"Just some errands. What about you?"

She hesitated for a moment before saying, "I stopped by the library to see what I could learn about Sutton Hall."

He fought the urge to frown. On the one hand it would make sense that she'd be interested in learning more about the place she intended to hold her wedding. On the other, someone with less up-front motives would probably do the same. The fact that she'd chosen to go into town to do her digging instead of asking people at Sutton Hall only raised his suspicions. "You didn't need to go into town for that. You could have asked anyone at the house. I'm sure they would have been happy to tell you anything you wanted to know."

"I'm so not sure about that. Other than Meredith, no one at Sutton Hall seems that talkative, and the place is still new to her, too."

"I hope no one's made you feel unwelcome," he said automatically, unable to keep a hint of dryness from the words.

Out of the corner of his eye, he saw her turn her head and look directly at him. "Do you?"

"We want every *bride* who comes to Sutton Hall to have a good experience for her special day," he said, pointedly emphasizing the relevant word.

"Or at least a better one than the first bride to come here?"

At the thought of Courtney Miller and what had happened to her, everything inside him went cold. "None of us want anything like that to happen ever again."

"Did you know Jacob Sutton used to sit out on the balcony overlooking the road leading up the mountain and just stare for hours, like he was still waiting for his wife to return?"

"No, I didn't know that," he said, already guessing where she was going with this.

"That's the same balcony that woman fell from, isn't it?"

As if she didn't already know. "Yes."

"It's kind of a strange coincidence."

"Not really. That balcony has the best view in the house. That's why Meredith chose that room for her. It's only understandable he would have chosen to sit there as well."

"I guess so," she said vaguely.

"It's just as much of a coincidence as your car breaking down on the same road his wife's went off of," he pointed out.

Adam sensed her tense slightly. "Is that where it happened?" she asked faintly.

"Not at that particular spot, I'm sure. It's not steep enough there for her car to sustain much damage if it went into the ditch. It was probably farther up the road, closer to where we are now."

She turned her head and peered out the window at her side, though it was unlikely she could see anything in the darkness. "How far are we from the house?"

"About two miles," he said. "You would have had quite a walk ahead of you. An even longer one if you'd decided to head back toward town. You're lucky I came along when I did."

"Hmm. Lucky," she said, as though she had reason to doubt that.

Of course, given their previous encounter, she might have reason not to want to spend too much time around him. But was it because she knew he was on to her, or because he'd been rude to her?

She ran her hand idly over the leather lining along the inside of the door. "By the way, nice car."

"It gets the job done."

"I'd say it does a lot better than that. Something like this couldn't have been cheap."

"Are you asking how much I paid for it?" he asked, amused by her audacity in spite of himself.

"No," she said with a faint smile. "I'm just guessing it means you were successful at whatever you did before you decided to start this wedding business at Sutton Hall."

"I was."

She turned that assessing gaze on him. He didn't even have to look directly at her to know it. He could feel it. "Yet you gave it up to open a wedding business in Vermont."

"It was important to Meredith." Adam shot her a look. "It *is* important to her. That's something I take very seriously. And I don't appreciate anyone wasting her time."

He might have expected her to proclaim the purity of her intentions here once again. She didn't, surveying him gravely with those startling green eyes.

"Your sister must mean a lot to you," she said.

"She does," he said firmly. "Remember that."

"Were the two of you always close?" she asked blandly, as if he hadn't spoken.

"Always," he confirmed. "I was six when Meredith was born. Our father worked a lot and wasn't around much, and our mother wasn't exactly the nurturing type, so I always watched out for her. All we really had was each other." Until she'd needed him most, he acknowledged bitterly. He hadn't been there for her then.

"She's lucky to have you," Jillian said softly.

The sentiment sounded genuine, but hearing it come from her, knowing that he couldn't really trust a word she said, sent a fresh wave of anger through him. "What about your family?" he challenged. "Why aren't they here with you?"

"I don't have any."

He didn't know if he should believe her. It could be a lie, like he suspected so many other things were that she'd told him, a ploy for his sympathy, to get him to back off. But something in the simple way she said it—without hesitation, without emotion—made him think she was telling the truth. "I'm sorry," he said, and was surprised to find he meant it.

"It's all right. I've had a long time to get used to it."

"Well, you won't have to be used to it much longer. Once you're married, you and your husband will be your own family."

"That's true."

I don't believe it is, he was tempted to reply, but it was clear she wasn't going to budge from that particular story anytime soon.

"You know, the other bride, Courtney Miller, didn't have any family, either. That was one reason she was here alone. The wedding was just going to be her, her groom and some of their closest friends. Just like you."

"I didn't know that," Jillian said after a beat, not slowly enough for him to tell if she was lying.

"Interesting coincidence."

"There seem to be a lot of those going around,"

she noted wryly. "It makes sense, though. It's a lot easier to have a wedding in an out-of-the-way place with a small wedding party than it would be when you have a lot of people who'd have to travel. And when you don't have a lot of family, it's only natural you'd want to do something extra special for the wedding." She paused again. "At least that's how I thought about it."

Adam almost shook his head. She had an explanation for everything, didn't she?

They fell back into silence. Adam did his best to focus on the road, but no matter how hard he tried, he found his gaze kept drifting back to her, unerringly drawn by the sight of her out of the corner of his eye.

He didn't know what it was about her that he found so compelling. She was beautiful, but it wasn't as though he hadn't met plenty of beautiful women in his lifetime. She was strong, but he'd encountered any number of strong women in the business world and gone toe-to-toe with them, and none of them had captured his attention like this. She was smart and quick-witted and fearless, all qualities shared by plenty of other people. But he'd never met the unique combination of those particular qualities that was Jillian Jones, and that made all the difference. And no matter how much he knew he should look away, he simply couldn't.

The appearance of lights up ahead provided a welcome distraction. Adam looked at the road to see they'd finally arrived back at Sutton Hall, the building looming in front of them, lights blazing from its many windows.

He almost sighed, a sense of contentment falling over him. A year ago when he'd first seen it, he never would have imagined a place this massive and imposing could feel like home. Yet it did, the feeling stronger than ever each time he found his way back to it.

He circled the driveway and pulled up directly in front of the house. By the time he got out and rounded the vehicle to her side, Jillian was already climbing out.

Closing the door, she turned to face him. "Thank you for the ride."

"You're welcome," he said. "You should call the rental company about your car."

"I will."

At the reminder of her vehicle, a flicker of worry passed over her features, and she looked vulnerable for a moment. He'd never seen her look that way before. Even when he'd confronted her last night in the tower bedroom and she'd stood there, dwarfed by the size of the room around her, the wind blowing against her, she hadn't seemed vulnerable. She'd exuded confidence. She didn't now.

He didn't like it. It looked wrong on her. The urge was there to reach out and say something comforting, to do what he could to erase that look from her eyes.

Which was foolish, of course. He managed to hold himself in check. Having her worried was exactly what he should want to get her to call off this lie he was convinced she was perpetuating.

He took a step toward her, forcing her to tilt her head back slightly to look up at him, and hardened his tone. "About what I said before… I wasn't kidding. Meredith is the only family I have in this world. I'm not going to let anyone hurt her. So if you are wasting her time or do anything to cause her grief, you will answer for it. I promise you that."

If he'd hoped to intimidate her, he saw immediately that he'd failed. The fire in her eyes sparked back to life. Her expression smoothed, and she raised her head with a stubborn jut of her chin.

He knew he should consider her defiance a bad sign, an indication she wasn't going to back down. But damn if it didn't look good on her.

"Just because I don't have any family doesn't mean I don't understand what it means to be willing to do anything for the people I care about."

Something in the words, in the way she said

them, struck an uneasy chord inside him. "So we understand each other."

"Absolutely," she shot back.

There didn't seem to be anything left to say. He waited for her to turn on her heel and storm into the house in a huff.

She didn't. She stood there, glaring up at him, eyes spitting fury. The moment went on. And he realized she didn't want to be the first to break or back down any more than he did.

The insight only stoked his own anger, and it was all he could do not to growl at her. The reaction startled him. He never came close to losing control of his emotions like that. But there was something about this woman… She really wouldn't give in the slightest. Not when it came to the truth. Not when it came to leaving here. Not even when it came to staring him down.

They stood there, gazes locked, the tension so thick he could almost feel it crackling in the air between them. Neither of them had moved. There was a little more than a foot between them, the same amount of space since he'd taken that step forward, but the distance seemed to shrink the longer they stood there, as though they were slowly drawing together.

The light from the house poured down over her face, illuminating every flawless line and beautiful feature, so much that she almost seemed to glow. Yet it was those blazing green eyes that drew him, radiating every ounce of fire she had burning inside, every inch of determination, every bit of *passion*... .

Suddenly anger wasn't the only thing he was feeling, and the emotion that had been slowly building deep inside finally burst forth.

Want. Pure, raw want.

There must have been a change in his gaze. He saw the instant she recognized it, her eyes flaring the tiniest bit. With surprise. With awareness.

Yet still she didn't move away. Still she stared into his eyes, hard and unblinking.

And the emotion radiating from her wasn't anger, either.

A purely masculine sense of triumph surged from deep in his gut as it registered.

No, not just anger.

It had been too long since he'd been with a woman. The past year he'd been so consumed with this place, not to mention fairly isolated up here trying to get it into shape, that he hadn't really had the time or the opportunity to seek out female company. That had to be it. This was just the effect of his unplanned celibacy taking its toll.

Except he hadn't reacted this way to the last bride to come here, hadn't felt anything for her.

Hadn't felt anything for anyone in longer than he could remember.

Yet here he was. Here *she* was.

It would be so simple to step forward and close the meager space that separated them, to pull her hard against him, to crush his mouth against hers, to see if her lips felt as soft and supple as they looked.

To see how she responded, if she'd have as much fire kissing him back as she had matching him word for word.

It could be incredible. He suspected it would be, every inch of his body taut with the drive, the need, to do it.

It would also be a mistake. That most of all.

And before he did anything he would end up regretting, he quickly turned and walked away.

ADAM STEPPED AWAY so suddenly Jillian felt a jolt of surprise that rocked her onto her heels. Trying to regain her equilibrium, she watched him stride away toward the side of the house, his back disappearing into the darkness.

She released a breath she hadn't realized she was holding, feeling strangely deflated even before she let it out. That wasn't what she'd thought was about to happen. She'd thought he'd been about to…

Kiss her. That's what she'd thought. That's what every female instinct she had said was coming.

What every deep-seated impulse had been wanting.

Which was crazy.

It was the last thing he should want to do, the last thing she should want him to.

So why did she feel so disappointed?

Jillian stared after him, contemplating the mystery that was Adam Sutton, even though he'd long since vanished from sight. He could be so harsh, so cold. But only when his sister was involved, she acknowledged. Only when it came to his family being threatened.

A man who cared that much about his sister that he would give up his career to take on something she wanted to do couldn't be all bad, could he?

She suddenly wanted more than anything for the answer to be no, even as part of her wondered if she had even less of a reason to trust him.

Was there a reason he was so protective of his sister? Emma had told her a lot about the staff at Sutton Hall, but Jillian still knew little about the Suttons themselves. If Meredith had been involved in Courtney's death, Jillian didn't doubt for a second Adam would do whatever he had to in order to protect her.

It had been Meredith's decision to put Courtney in that room, Jillian thought, tucking away that piece of information. It made sense, and she'd suspected as much, but it was good to know for sure. Now she just had to figure out if it meant anything.

Exhaling deeply, she fought the urge to press a hand to her throbbing head. All these doubts and suspicions about everyone here were exhausting. She wished there was someone she could confide in, someone she could trust....

Wished it was him...

Jillian shook off the ridiculous thought. She'd known what she was signing up for when she decided to come here. She had to keep on her guard against everyone here, no matter how wearing it was on her.

Especially the ones who might be interfering with her instincts in different ways.

Even as the thought passed through her mind, she felt a prickling at the nape of her neck, an entirely different instinct kicking in. She recognized the sensation, the feeling undeniable.

She was being watched.

Curious, she turned and peered up at the building.

The multitude of windows stared back at her, some of them blazing with light, some gaping with emptiness. She didn't spot anyone in any of them looking back at her.

Unease creeping along her skin, she glanced around the area. Her unseen watcher didn't have to be in the house. Whoever it was could be somewhere out here.

She saw nothing in the long shadows surrounding the edge of the driveway and the ends of the house, heard nothing but the faint whisper of the leaves in the trees, stirred by the night wind.

Felt the intensity of that unseen gaze boring into her, as strongly as if it were physically touching her. And there was nothing remotely friendly in the feeling.

Whoever it was, she clearly wasn't going to spot them. And she suddenly knew without a doubt that they didn't want to be seen.

Trying her best not to show her unease, even as the sensation of being watched weighed down on her more than ever, she started for the door to the house. Once she was inside, she should be out of the watcher's sight. Not to mention she needed to call the rental company about her car. Hopefully they'd be able to repair it, or bring her a replacement. Without the vehicle, she was effectively trapped here, on her own.

In a place that was rapidly feeling more dangerous to her by the moment.

NARROWED EYES FOLLOWED Jillian Jones's retreat into the house until she disappeared from view.

Before she did, she glanced around herself one more time, at the house, at the outside area.

She knew someone was watching her, had been trying to see who it was.

She didn't know it was too late. The scene that had damned her had already been witnessed.

Revulsion churned at the memory—and what it meant.

Somehow she'd come back with Adam, even though they'd left for town separately. They'd been alone together in his car—at least as long as the ride back. Maybe even longer…

However long it had been, something seemed to have happened between them. That moment they'd shared after climbing out of the car was entirely too intimate for two people with nothing going on between them.

The way he'd stood there, just a little closer than was normal, staring down at her, saying nothing…

The way she'd looked up at him. With intensity. With interest.

With lust.

The sexual attraction between them was undeniable, obvious even from a distance.

And disgusting from any angle.

A woman who was getting married had no business standing that close to a man who wasn't her husband-to-be, not like that, not for that long.

She should have stepped away, made it clear it wasn't appropriate, that she wasn't interested.

But she hadn't.

Jillian Jones was another one, a slut who had no right to put on that white dress, to take vows she didn't mean, just like the other woman.

She would have to be stopped, too.

Chapter Seven

"Oh, Jillian, I forgot to ask. What did you think of Hawthorne?"

Jillian glanced up from her plate to find Meredith smiling at her from across the dining room table. From the moment Rosie had served the meal, Meredith had been making a valiant attempt to keep a conversation going. No easy feat since she and Jillian were the only ones speaking.

Adam sat at the head of the table to Jillian's right. Ever since he'd entered the room he'd mostly avoided looking at her. Every once in a while she'd sensed him glance in her direction, the feeling of his gaze now familiar, his focus hard and intense. She'd studiously avoided looking at him, either, the memory of their encounter in the driveway too fresh. And after a moment he'd look away.

"It's lovely," she said in answer to Meredith's question. "Even smaller than I realized but really pretty and charming."

"I know it's small and less geared to visitors than a lot of towns in the area," Meredith said. "But if you want to explore further or think your guests would, there are plenty of other nearby towns and places to see within driving distance I could point you toward."

"Well, I'm glad I had a chance to explore it, but I'll probably stick a little closer to Sutton Hall the rest of my time here."

"Especially since your rental car seems to have broken down," Adam observed.

It was the first time he'd spoken since they'd sat down for dinner. The sound of his voice sent an unexpected frisson of shock through her. His tone was mild, but the words sounded vaguely insinuating. As though he thought she'd done something to disable the car.

She forced the sweetest smile she could manage. "Fortunately they already brought a replacement."

"So you could leave anytime you like," he said slowly.

"If I wanted to. I just don't think I'll see the need."

"And you never know when something else might happen to the new car."

"Why would it?" she challenged him.

His lips curved slowly, the smile looking more like a smirk. "I can't imagine."

"What did the rental company say when they picked up the car?" Meredith interjected, shooting her brother a look.

"They couldn't immediately tell what was wrong with it, but they're going to check it out."

"Good. Well, I'm glad they were able to take care of it so quickly. And that Adam came along when he did so you weren't stranded out there," Meredith added after a beat.

Jillian figured she was better off not commenting on that. Adam didn't, either, lowering his gaze to his plate.

Trying to put him out of her mind for the moment, Jillian turned her attention to the fourth person at the table. Grace sat to Meredith's right, giving Jillian a prime view of the woman. Jillian had been mildly curious about the fact that the housekeeper had eaten dinner with them the night before, when none of the rest of the staff had. Rosie had served the meal, with Ed helping her, as they did tonight. Ray and Zack were nowhere to be found, presumably handling their own dinner arrangements. That just left Grace.

Last night she'd chimed in to the discussion, describing some of the features of the house as they talked about the wedding plans. Tonight, though, she seemed to have little to say. Of course, given the tension hanging over the meal, she might just think it was better to keep her mouth shut.

The woman certainly didn't act like a housekeeper. Sitting stiffly in her chair, her head held high, she had the regal bearing of a queen. Jillian almost thought she looked as though she belonged at the head of the table.

Given a few of the looks Jillian caught her slipping Adam, she wouldn't have been surprised if Grace thought so, too.

"So, Grace," Jillian said as casually as possible. "I think Meredith said you've been here for almost thirty years?"

The housekeeper nodded, meeting Jillian's eyes with a small, polite smile. "Yes, that's right."

"So you must have known Kathleen Sutton."

"Mrs. Sutton is the one who hired me. I came here when she did."

"Oh, really?" Jillian said as if she didn't know. "Where are you from originally?"

For the first time, Grace hesitated, the pause long enough to be noticeable. "Philadelphia," she said.

Jillian wondered about her reluctance. Was it that she simply didn't want to share anything personal, or was there something particular about that piece of information? "Is that where Mrs. Sutton was from, too?"

"Yes." Grace quickly turned her attention back to her plate.

"I'd love to hear more about her and Jacob. His love for her is so inspiring. It would be great to find out more about them as a couple."

Jillian almost wondered if she imagined the way Grace seemed to tense, the reaction so slight it was nearly imperceptible. "They loved each other very much. They were very happy here."

"What was she like?"

Grace appeared to consider the question. "She was very kind," she finally said, her voice softening in a way Jillian had never heard before. "Quite beautiful as you could see from the portrait in the main hall. Generous. Well liked. Well loved. And, I suppose…irreplaceable, really."

It was a strange choice of words, especially toward someone who'd been her employer. *Irreplaceable.* It almost seemed to indicate attempts had been made to replace her and come up short.

Studying the woman's downcast eyes, it occurred to Jillian that, as the head of the household, Grace herself had essentially been Kathleen Sutton's replacement. In every way but one.

And that was when Jillian knew.

Grace had loved Jacob Sutton.

Her choice of that word and the way she said it told Jillian everything she needed to know. It made sense. Grace had stayed here for thirty years in this isolated location, taking care of him, never leaving to have a family or life of her own away from here, away from him. Loyalty to her employer could only explain so much.

Jillian remembered the way Grace had been staring at the portrait of Jacob Sutton yesterday. Was that the reason for the look on her face, because she'd been in love with him? If it was true, it would seem her affections hadn't been returned, especially if Jacob had spent his final years sitting on that balcony, thinking about his late wife.

A Sutton man loves forever.

Maybe a romantic sentiment to some. But not for someone in love with a Sutton man who would forever love someone else.

"What about you?" Jillian asked. "Do you have any family?"

"No," Grace said flatly.

"Thirty years is a long time. You never wanted to live anywhere else? Try a different job?" *Love someone else, especially since Jacob Sutton was gone?*

Grace lifted her head. Her face never shifted, the slight, enigmatic smile still on her lips, her expression as cool and composed as ever. No one else in the room would have seen the change. Only Jillian, who was staring directly into Grace's eyes, could have seen the hardness that entered her stare as Grace looked back at her with a sudden coldness that chilled her to the bone. "This is my home."

"And we're glad to have her," Meredith said finally into the silence that followed.

"Of course you are," Jillian said. "I'm sorry," she told Grace. "I didn't mean to pry."

The woman smiled thinly, meeting Jillian's eyes with a look that said she knew perfectly well that was exactly what Jillian had been doing.

The door to the kitchen suddenly swung open, and Rosie emerged, carrying a tray with four bowls on it. Ed followed close behind her. "Who's ready for dessert?"

"I'm not sure any of us have room after that meal," Meredith said with a smile. "Rosie, you outdid yourself."

Rosie practically glowed at the praise. "Well, no meal is truly finished without dessert, so you'd better have room. I made a nice rice pudding."

The husband-and-wife team began moving around the table, Ed taking the used plates and utensils and placing them on the tray he carried, Rosie following closely behind and setting a bowl and clean spoon in front of each of them.

"I do apologize, though," Rosie said. "I was going to bake a cake, but Ed didn't come back from town with the sugar I asked for."

"I'm afraid I forgot," Ed said lightly, a hint of sheepishness in his voice as he took Jillian's plate.

"Even though I gave you a list so you wouldn't," Rosie returned.

"It's fine," Jillian said quickly. "It's been a long time since I had pudding. It's a nice change of pace."

"Sad to say, it's from a mix," Rosie said with a sniff of disdain. "But sometimes we just have to make do with what we have."

"It's not a problem," Meredith said. "I'm sure this is great, and Jillian will be eating plenty of cake soon enough. Right, Jillian?"

"Right," Jillian said, forcing a chuckle.

Rosie placed a bowl and a fresh spoon in front of her. Jillian automatically picked up the spoon. As she raised it to the bowl, she glanced up and across the table.

Grace was watching her, her gaze intense and unwavering. Jillian nearly shivered.

As soon as Jillian's eyes met hers, Grace smiled thinly again before lowering her gaze to her bowl.

Jillian continued to stare at the woman for a moment, considering what lay behind that placid exterior and cold stare.

This is my home, Jillian heard in the back of her mind.

And she suddenly wondered exactly what Grace would do if there was someone in her home she didn't want here.

BY THE TIME Jillian made it back to her room a few hours after dinner, she was ready to turn in early. Even if she hadn't gotten little sleep the night before, the endless day had left her exhausted. Barely able to keep her eyes open as she prepared for bed, she locked the door of the suite, blocking out the rest of Sutton Hall and its inhabitants, and eagerly climbed beneath the covers. Her head had barely hit the pillow before she was asleep.

She couldn't escape Sutton Hall even in her dreams. It rose up in her mind, even more beautiful and unsettling, lush and grim, than it was in real life.

She dreamed she was wandering its halls, the corridors long and unending, thick with shadows. They seemed to go on forever, and no matter where she turned she couldn't escape them. Emma's words seemed to fill the air, echoing all around her.

Be careful....

Watch out for yourself....

Just in case...

She dreamed of Courtney, dressed in her wedding gown, begging her for help. She floated backward down the shadowy halls, as though being dragged away by unseen hands. All the while, she reached out to Jillian, her arms outstretched, her face contorted in terror, her mouth open in a silent scream. Jillian tried to go to her, but Courtney drifted down the halls away from her, always out of reach, her eyes bright with fear—and what seemed to Jillian was a hint of betrayal. Until finally she disappeared entirely, leaving Jillian chasing after nothing.

She dreamed of Meredith and Grace, of Rosie and Ed, of Ray and Zack. As she wandered down the dark, endless hallways, she passed them, again and again. They were always watching her silently, their expressions intense and unreadable, their eyes following her wherever she went. She tried to run, to escape them, through the never-ending maze of halls. But no matter where she turned, they were there, their faces growing darker, more sinister with every glimpse. She ran faster, harder, desperate to get away from them, until she ran straight into—

Adam Sutton, the lights from the house shining down on one side of his face, leaving the other shrouded in darkness.

He didn't touch her, didn't say anything. He simply stood there, looking down at her.

She stared up into that compelling face, the expression on it as cool and remote as ever, searching those impenetrable eyes for any hint of what he was thinking. The longer she looked, the less it seemed that she saw. Instead it felt as if she was losing herself, falling hopelessly into his mysterious gaze. Her heart pounding, her lungs tightening, she tried to look away, only to find she couldn't. She could only stare into those bottomless eyes that revealed nothing. They seemed to consume her, pulling the very life out of her, the feeling overpowering. It was almost as though she was choking, suffocating, completely unable to breathe. And all the while he simply stood there, watching her, as her terror climbed higher and higher.

Her preservation instinct kicked in, and she realized this was only a dream. She could wake up. She needed to—

Wake up!

The image of him vanished. She stared into blackness, unable to see anything. But still she couldn't breathe. The feeling was worse than ever, the darkness absolute, her lungs clutching, screaming for air—

Wake up!

And then somewhere in the panicked recesses of her mind it hit her. She *was* awake. Her eyes were wide open. She just couldn't see anything. She could feel the mattress beneath her, the sheets around her, far more sharply than she had in the dream.

This wasn't a dream. It was real. She *was* choking, suffocating. Something was on her face, pressing down, cutting off the air.

The pillow. The pillow was over her face.

She threw out her hands, clawing at whatever was forcing the pillow down. Her fingers made contact, gripping whatever they encountered.

Wrists. Arms. They began to thrash, resist, as hard as she was. The pressure on her face increased.

A person. It was a person. Someone was holding the pillow down, trying to suffocate her, trying to *kill* her.

She fought harder, even as she felt her body weakening from the lack of air, her lungs seizing, her limbs tensing—

She lashed out with her arms and legs, her hands beating against the ones holding the pillow, her feet flailing to make contact with any part of the attacker. She threw her full weight from side to side, twisting her neck, trying to break away from the pillow just enough for one precious breath of air.

And then it happened.

An instant later, the pillow disappeared. Cool, fresh air wafted over her face.

She sucked in a breath with a loud, ragged

gasp that filled her ears. Her lungs were so tight she could barely get any of that precious air into them. Jerking upright, she breathed in again, and again. Even as she did it, she peered into the darkness, willing her vision to clear, so she could see who—

The light. She needed the light.

Lunging for the bedside table, she fumbled for the lamp, her fingertips searching the darkness as desperately as her eyes did. Finally, thankfully, her fingers made contact with the knob. She gave it a furious twist, automatically jerking her head from side to side as a pale pool of light flared to life, revealing the room, and—

She froze, her heart in her throat, shock rocketing through her.

There was no one there.

She gaped in disbelief, jerking her head to take in the room, seeking out every inch of the space. The result was the same.

The room was empty, as peaceful and undisturbed as it had been when she'd gone to bed, the door firmly closed.

She was alone.

No. She almost shook her head in denial. It wasn't possible. Whoever it was had to be hiding, maybe waiting for her to lower her guard so they could burst out and attack again.

The thought instantly spurred her into motion.

She shoved the covers aside and jumped to her feet. Scanning the space for the nearest possible weapon, she spotted a fireplace poker on a stand next to the hearth. She raced for it, fully expecting to be intercepted at any moment. When she finally had it in hand, she gripped it in front of her with both fists and considered the room, looking for anyplace someone could be hiding.

Her gaze fell on the bathroom door.

The bathroom.

The door was slightly ajar. Had she left it like that? She didn't remember. The attacker could be in there, might not have been able to shut the door.

She wasted no time second-guessing herself. Crossing to the door in two strides, she raised the poker in her arms, drew back her leg and kicked the door in.

It flew inward with a bang, crashing against the inside wall. She waited for a cry of surprise, of someone lurching out of the way, for any hint someone was in there.

Nothing.

Inching forward, she reached in carefully with one hand and flipped on the light.

The room was empty.

The discovery only stoked the agitation burning in her gut, her chest tightening until it felt as though she was running out of air again. It wasn't possible. The intruder had to be here somewhere. Unless they'd somehow managed to get out the door…

Turning on her heel, she marched over to the entrance to the suite.

The door was still locked.

She really was alone.

But she hadn't been. It didn't matter that she didn't see anyone now. She knew it, certainty pounding through her veins as hard as the adrenaline still filling her body.

Someone had been in the room with her, attacked her in her sleep and escaped before she could turn on the light. She didn't know how, but somehow they'd managed to do it, vanishing into thin air.

Almost, she thought as a whisper of unease crawled along her skin, like a ghost.

Except it hadn't been a ghost, she told herself firmly. Whoever it was had been very real.

She looked around the vast suite, the room no longer seeming remotely safe. She had a momentary impulse to leave, but that didn't exactly seem like a better choice. If the intruder was no longer inside, he—or she—was somewhere out there now.

She considered her options. There seemed to be only one.

Climbing back into bed, Jillian pushed the

pillows up against the headboard and propped herself up against them. There wasn't much chance she was going to get any more sleep tonight, not with the uncertainty of what had just happened clouding her brain, not with the remembered terror of those moments still thrumming through her.

Laying the fireplace poker across her lap, she sat there, eyes still searching the room for the intruder she knew had been there, and waited desperately for morning to come.

Chapter Eight

Someone had tried to kill her.

Jillian had plenty of time to consider what had happened to her through the darkest hours of the night before dawn finally broke. And of all the conclusions she'd reached, that one loomed the largest.

Someone had tried to kill her.

She knew it in her bones. She remembered the feeling of the weight of the pillow against her face, the shape of the arms beneath her fingers, too vividly not to know they'd been real.

The thought ran over and over again in her head, and every time it sent a fresh jolt of anger through her. It was all she could do not to glance around the dining room table at the others seated over breakfast, hoping to catch a glimpse of a guilty expression or someone looking back at her too intently, or avoiding her gaze too deliberately.

But she didn't expect anyone to do anything that obvious. More important, she wasn't going to let them think they'd spooked her, or that she even suspected what had happened wasn't just a dream. They might wonder why she didn't try to leave if she thought she'd been attacked, and she wasn't going anywhere.

Because now there wasn't a doubt in her mind that what happened to Courtney had been no accident.

She'd been murdered.

Jillian's stomach clenched with certainty, nearly rejecting the few bites of breakfast she'd choked down. She didn't know why the attacker had targeted her. Was it because they knew who she was, why she was here, and figured she had to be stopped from asking questions? Or had they come after her for the same reason they'd come after Courtney, something to do with brides in this place? Either way, it couldn't be a coincidence that the first bride to come to Sutton Hall had died a mysterious death and the second was attacked in the middle of the night. The events had to be connected. And the most reasonable conclusion was that Courtney had met with foul play, exactly as Jillian had figured.

There was another connection as well. Someone had managed to get into her locked room without detection. The police said one of the reasons it seemed clear Courtney must have fallen was because the door to her room had been locked. Adam had told them he'd unlocked the door when she hadn't responded to any summons that morning, found the room empty and the balcony doors open. Jillian had had her doubts about the story, but now she had to wonder if it was true. She knew firsthand that a locked door wasn't enough to keep someone out in Sutton Hall, or to prevent a vicious attack. Was that what happened to Courtney?

If they'd used a key to get in, she would have heard them relocking it, even if she hadn't heard the door shut. There was only one other explanation she could think of for how someone had managed to get in and out of the locked room.

There had to be another, hidden entrance of some kind.

She'd done a cursory search for it that morning, but had come up empty. Which hadn't killed her conviction that it had to be there.

Preparing her words carefully, she raised her head to look at Grace. "So, Grace, I was wondering about something. When I think of an old mansion like this, I always think of secret passageways and hidden doors, stuff like that. Does Sutton Hall have any of those?"

At the other side of the table, Grace went very still, her mouth thinning in a tight smile. "I'm afraid not. Those types of things are only found in fiction, or if not, the builders of Sutton Hall weren't nearly so creative."

She was lying. Even if Jillian wasn't positive the passages had to exist, the woman's body language gave her away. She was trying to remain casual, all while her neck and shoulders had tensed just enough to indicate she wasn't.

"Secret passageways?" Adam asked.

Jillian slowly turned her head to look at him, trying to forget how he'd looked in her dream last night. He watched her through narrowed eyes, his skepticism clear.

She shrugged lightly. "You have to admit, it's something most people would be curious about. Can't blame me for asking."

He raised a brow, as if to ask, *Can't I?*

She simply smiled back at him, taking a perverse enjoyment from the way his expression darkened in response, as though he suspected she was up to something. No surprise there.

Then, as she stared at that coolly considering face, another thought occurred to her, killing that momentary pleasure.

Could he be the one who'd attacked her?

No, a voice in the back of her mind replied, rejecting the idea immediately. As soon as she did, she had to question her reaction. Did she really think it hadn't been him, or did she just not want to believe it?

As she took in that dark steady gaze and felt a nervous flutter deep in her belly in response, she had to admit she didn't know.

"You're right, of course," Meredith interjected into the silence, her voice tight. "It would be a great marketing gimmick if this place came complete with secret passages. Maybe we should look and see if we can find any."

Me first. "Maybe," Jillian agreed.

Even as she said it, she shot a glance at Grace. The woman's head remained bowed, her attention on her plate, but Jillian didn't miss the way her lips thinned into a tense, unhappy line, or how she seemed to have paled.

Grace didn't like the idea at all.

Jillian's certainty only grew, and she had to resist the urge to smile. She was right.

Now she just had to prove it.

CLAIMING SHE HAD an upset stomach, Jillian headed back to her room right after breakfast. As soon as she reached it, she began to consider where the hidden door could be. The attacker had managed to get out of the room between the time when she'd fought them off and when she'd turned on the lamp, so the entrance had to be relatively close to the bed, near enough that they could duck back through it and shut it again quickly. She eyed the wall next to the bed, figuring it had to be somewhere along there.

She didn't immediately spot anything out of the ordinary. It appeared to be nothing more than a plain wall. But of course a secret passageway would hardly be secret if it was obvious where the entrance was.

Stepping forward, she pressed her ear to the wall and began tapping along it, listening carefully for an echoing sound that could indicate the presence of an empty space on the other side. She made it all the way from the corner nearest the door to the edge of the bed, but didn't hear a thing. The wall sounded completely solid.

That didn't necessarily mean anything, she thought resolutely. The wall still might be thick enough to muffle the sound.

If there was some kind of door in the wall, there had to be a way to open it, assuming it wasn't only from the other side. Hoping that wasn't the case, she reached forward and pressed her fingers along the wallpaper, searching for any kind of button or latch, or even an indentation in the wall that would indicate the outline of a door.

She slowly, painstakingly began to go over the wall, starting at the top and working her way all along it, then dropping a little lower and making her way back.

She'd done several passes and was in the middle of the wall, her fingers at about shoulder level, when she finally felt something. It was so faint her fingertips nearly passed over it. Some vague instinct made her stop and retrace it, to confirm she hadn't imagined it.

It was a rectangular outline, roughly the size of an electrical outlet cover, though she didn't think that was what it was. It didn't protrude from the wall at all, but seemed to be part of the wall itself, as though carved into it. Touching the shape gingerly, she tried to figure out why it was there and what it could be. She didn't doubt that it had to be something, noticing that it perfectly aligned with the pattern on the wallpaper, which formed a rectangular shape right on top of it. It didn't stand out from the rest of the pattern, but if someone knew the rectangle was there, that spot on the pattern would offer a clear indication where to find it.

Without thinking about it, she pushed in on it.

A large section of the wall abruptly swung toward her the slightest bit, like a door suddenly ajar.

Which was exactly what it was, she realized. The protruding section of wall was roughly the size and shape of a regular door, only lacking a standard doorknob. It had released with near silence. It was so quiet she wasn't surprised she hadn't heard it last night over the pounding of her heart and her desperate breathing.

Rising to stand, she ran her fingers along the open edge in amazement. She'd looked at exactly that spot and hadn't noticed anything. She never would have known it was there. Even the spot she'd pushed was completely ingrained in the wall, making it utterly unnoticeable unless someone was specifically looking for it or knew where to find it.

Reaching out eagerly, she grabbed the edge in two hands and pulled it open. It moved easily. When she'd managed to create an opening several feet wide she stopped and looked inside.

Another wall lay directly in front of her, and in it was the outline of a rectangular shape. Another door. The next room over was the one in the southeast tower on this floor.

She looked over to see a thin set of stairs leading upward on her left, continuing downward on her right. A staircase, she thought, wonder bubbling through her. The passageway was a staircase between the tower and the rooms next to it.

For a moment she could only stand there and take it in, amazement spiraling through her. It was exactly what she'd expected. But believing it had to be there was different from seeing an actual hidden passageway in an old mansion in the flesh.

There didn't appear to be any lights that she could see, maybe not surprising since the manor—and the passages—had been built before the days of electricity. While the rest of the mansion had been upgraded, it didn't appear anyone had bothered with these.

More thankful than ever that she'd brought her flashlight, she grabbed it and stepped into the passageway. There was no time to waste. She wanted to confirm where it led, and see if there was any way to tell who'd been in here last.

Moving forward, Jillian shined the flashlight around the inside of the passage. The tunnel was maybe eight feet high and three feet wide, much thinner than a typical hallway, but big enough that an average-sized person could walk down it easily. The walls were plain and unpainted. The floors were made of stone, and on them—

She froze, aiming the flashlight on the ground and looking closer. They appeared to be covered with a layer of dust, noticeable only because it had been disturbed by—

Footprints. There were footprints in the dust.

The passages had been used recently.

Proof, she thought, triumph racing through her.

Jillian hesitated for a moment, suddenly unsure whether she wanted to disturb the evidence that someone had been here. But this might be her only chance to explore. She couldn't waste it.

Resolutely, she turned left and started up the steps.

The stairwell wound upward, no doubt following the tower. She could see only a few feet in front of her at a time, the wall constantly curving before her. Jillian imagined a servant navigating these passages over a hundred years ago, a candle in hand, with only the flickering flame to light the cold stone walls. Or maybe the Suttons themselves, creeping about in the walls of their own mansion, for who-only-knew what purpose....

The stairs came to an abrupt end at a short landing. Based on the height of the ceiling above her, Jillian assumed she'd reached the top of the tower.

Again there were the outlines of two doors on either side of her. The one on the left had to lead into the bedroom directly above hers. And the one on the right—

The bedroom at the top of this tower.

Spotting a lever next to the door, Jillian automatically reached for it. She hesitated briefly, wondering about the possibility that someone was in the room on the other side. It didn't seem likely. As far as she knew it wasn't occupied, and what were the chances someone would be cleaning it right now?

She pulled the lever.

The door unlatched. A thrill of excitement racing through her, she put her shoulder to it and began pushing it in. It only took a few inches for Jillian to see exactly what she'd expected.

It wasn't exactly the same as the room in the other tower where Courtney had stayed, but the layout was nearly identical, only reversed. And if there was a hidden passageway in this tower, Jillian had no doubt there was one in the other, most likely in all of them.

This was it, she thought, anger and certainty hardening into a tight knot in the pit of her stomach. This was how somebody had gotten to Courtney. She probably hadn't even seen them coming. They'd come in through the passageway unannounced, managed to get her to the balcony and then—

Jillian swallowed hard at the images that played out in her head.

The only remaining mystery was whether she'd been dead before she'd gone off the balcony—or after.

Wincing at the thought, Jillian turned away from the scene. She didn't want to think about that now.

She would love to go back to the other tower

to confirm it, but she didn't know if Adam still had the sensor in place. She couldn't have him catching her there, couldn't let him know she was aware of the hidden stairs. There was far more she needed to explore.

Grabbing the latch on the inside of the wall-door, she yanked it hard and pulled it shut. All right. So she knew the tower bedroom and her own were both accessible from the tunnel. Now to see where else it led.

As she made her way back down the stairs to the second floor, she remembered that Meredith was the one who'd put Courtney in the tower bedroom and Jillian in the room she was in. Just another coincidence, or had Meredith known exactly what she was doing to give someone— herself?—access to her guests?

Jillian thought back to Meredith's reaction at breakfast. She hadn't given any indication she knew about the passages, but then, Jillian had mostly been paying attention to Grace's reactions.

More questions, she thought with a grimace. Every time she found an answer, it only led to more puzzles. All she could do was keep moving forward and hope she eventually arrived at the ultimate answers she needed.

She passed the second floor, where the door to

her room was still slightly ajar, and continued on. The stairwell spiraled downward into the dark.

Another door finally appeared up ahead in the beam of her flashlight. It was on the inner wall of the stairwell. She figured that must mean it led to a room inside the tower. At the same time the stairs continued going downward beyond it.

She hadn't been on this side of the house in the first floor, had no idea what room could be in the tower here. She needed to know, though. Needed to learn what room this was to figure out how her attacker had most likely accessed the passageway to get to her.

Only one way to find out.

Loosening the latch, she opened the door, then began pushing it in. With any luck, this room would be empty, too.

Once she'd created a large enough gap, she straightened. She caught a glimpse of a wall full of books. From what she could see, it was a library of some kind, maybe a study or office....

She took a couple steps in, then came to an abrupt stop.

It appeared her luck had run out.

Adam stood a few feet in front of her, eyes wide, his mouth open slightly. There was a desk behind him, and she realized in an instant she'd been right. This was an office.

His office.

He looked shocked—because he really hadn't known about the passageways, or just because of her sudden appearance from them?

"What the hell—?" He stared first at her, then at the gap she'd opened in the wall. "What are you doing in there?"

"Just exploring these secret passages. You know, the ones that don't exist?"

"How—? What—?" Evidently unable to settle on the question he wanted to ask most, he finally clamped his mouth shut and gave his head a hard shake. "Get out of there. I don't know how you managed to find that, but I can't have you wandering around in there. It might not be safe."

"It's fine," she said patiently.

"You can't know that for sure, and I certainly can't. God only knows how long it's been since anyone's been in there, what kind of shape it's in. If anything happened—"

Clearly arguing wasn't going to get her anywhere, and she wasn't about to let him stop her. Without listening to another word, she spun around and ducked back into the passage.

"Hey!"

His voice echoed from behind her, but she didn't stop moving, continuing onward. She'd made it down half a dozen stairs when she felt him coming up behind her. She braced herself for him to grab her and make her stop.

He didn't, as he caught up and fell into step behind her. She sensed him glancing around them.

"You can barely see anything in here."

"That's what the flashlight is for," she pointed out.

"And of course wandering around in a hidden passage you know nothing about with only a flashlight is perfectly safe."

"I'm getting by well enough."

"You know, this *is* my house," he said darkly.

"Well, then I'd think you'd like to get to know it better, because clearly there's a lot you don't know about it."

There was a beat of silence, and she could practically hear him grinding his teeth. "Is this why you came here? Because you wanted to look for secret passages?"

"No, this is just something I thought of today," she said truthfully.

"Uh-huh," he said, his disbelief obvious. "And what were you hoping to find if you did locate these hidden pathways?"

"Isn't that enough? Actual secret passages? They're not exactly something you see every day. If anything, you should be thanking me for something that will draw a lot more interest to this place and that your guests will love to see."

"That's just what we need. People wandering around inside the walls unsupervised. Never mind the possible safety hazard, there's no telling where these passages even go."

"All the more reason to explore them, don't you think—?"

Her foot suddenly slipped, flying out from under her. She hurtled forward, the flashlight tumbling out of her hand, the ground rushing up to meet her—

Something caught her right arm, breaking her fall, bringing her to an abrupt halt. She was whipped around, colliding with something hard and solid and immovable.

Breathless, she raised her head. It didn't help. She couldn't see anything, the flashlight and its faint glow somewhere on the floor behind her. It didn't matter. She knew whose hand was on her arm, whose body she was pressed against, even as she processed what had happened.

She'd slipped. He'd caught her.

As she peered up, trying to catch even the faintest glimpse of his face, she sensed him looking down at her.

"Are you okay?" he asked. The low rumble of his voice rolled over her like a caress, making her shudder in response.

She immediately knew he'd felt it, his body tensing slightly. He didn't say anything, and she realized he was probably still waiting for her response.

She managed a nod, only realizing a heart-beat later that he couldn't see it. "Yes, I'm fine."

She waited, expecting him to release his hold on her.

He didn't. His hand remained clasped around her arm, not too tight, but secure, and undeniably there. It wasn't the tightness of his hold she felt. It was the heat of his fingers against her flesh, the texture of his skin on hers, the coiled strength in his grip.

"Do you have your feet under you?" he asked, his voice even softer, and she nearly trembled again.

She flexed her feet, checking her bearings. The ground was solid beneath her. "Yes."

His fingers instantly popped open, letting her go. The action was so abrupt she might have rocked back on her heels if he hadn't let her steady herself beforehand.

She felt him lean back slightly. "Like I said, it's not safe in here."

You might be right about that. She turned away to retrieve the flashlight. It lay a few feet away, and she immediately realized why she'd stumbled. The stairs had ended, the ground leveling out. She'd been so distracted by their conversation she hadn't even noticed. "I tripped. It happens."

"Not in my secret passageways, you don't. As

I'm sure you remember, we've had some experience lately with women coming to Sutton Hall and...falling."

Jillian could tell from the edge in his words that he was baiting her, all too accurately, as it was. At the moment, the reminder was a welcome one. She needed to get a grip and keep in mind exactly why she'd come here. She didn't have time to be distracted by anything.

Or anyone.

Picking up the flashlight, she turned back to face him, illuminating the space between them. "I guess your concern does make a certain amount of sense when you put it like that," she conceded.

"Good. Let's get out of here."

"Do you want to go back up?" she asked, nodding toward the way they'd just come down.

"Let's not risk the stairs again. It'll probably be faster just to find the nearest exit down here. I'm sure there has to be one."

"I'm sure," Jillian murmured. She suspected there were exits all over the place, the passages offering access to any number of rooms in the house.

She shined her flashlight ahead of them, revealing a long, straight corridor that stretched on beyond the reach of the beam. They slowly moved down it. Contrary to their best guess, there didn't appear to be any doors along it. The walls were bare and seemingly unending.

"Is this the basement?" she asked.

"It has to be, but I don't recognize this hallway. We must still be within the walls."

The longer they walked, the more those walls seemed to close in on them. Jillian swallowed hard, unsure if the hallway was really narrowing or if it just felt that way. She was almost surprised he didn't suggest they turn back after all, but maybe he felt they had to be closer to the exit than the stairs at this point. All the while, she was more aware than ever of his presence just behind her, an arm's length away.

Finally, when it seemed as if the corridor truly would go on forever, another set of stairs appeared at the end of the flashlight's beam. The sight was so faint she couldn't be sure she wasn't imagining it at first. But the closer she came to them, the clearer it became that the stairs were real. They led up just one level to another door.

There was an exit after all. She felt Adam relax slightly behind her. Relief climbing in her throat, she started moving a little faster.

Reaching the steps, she took them two at a time. And then the door was there, right in front of her. She came to a stop, automatically reaching for the latch to release it.

"Let me—" Adam started to say.

"I've got it," she said, pushing the door inward before he could try to take her place.

It took her a moment to recognize the room that greeted her. It was the kitchen. The panel had opened into one of the side walls in Sutton Hall's massive kitchen.

Stepping into the room, Jillian immediately saw it wasn't empty, either. Rosie, Ed and Grace stood around the main island talking. None of them noticed her entrance at first. Only when Adam exited the passage behind her, his footsteps heavy on the hardwood floor, did they look up.

Ed's eyebrows shot up. Rosie's mouth formed an O of surprise. But it was Grace's face Jillian zeroed in on as the housekeeper took in their dusty, disheveled appearance with rapidly growing horror.

"Hello, Grace," Adam said grimly. "I think we need to talk."

Chapter Nine

Adam had to give Grace credit. By the time she stood in his office facing him and Meredith, she'd regained her composure, looking them straight in the eye as though she didn't have anything to regret or hide.

"Why didn't you tell us about the passages?" he asked bluntly.

"I didn't know if you would want me to reveal such a thing to a guest and haven't had a chance to speak with either of you privately about it since then."

"We've been here almost a year. You've had plenty of time to tell us about the passages."

"I apologize for the oversight."

Adam didn't believe for a second it was simply something she'd neglected to tell them. No, she'd purposely chosen not to. He studied her closely. In the past year he'd come to know her as being exceedingly competent and highly organized. But he realized he had never really gotten to know the woman herself, who she was, what made her tick.

Still, there was one thing he was fairly certain about at the moment. "You don't like us being here, do you?"

Grace didn't even blink. "It's your property. That was what Jacob wanted."

It wasn't the first time she'd referred to the previous owner of Sutton Hall by his first name. It had never struck Adam as unusual—everyone who'd been here for years called him Jacob—but for some reason, the way she said it sounded more personal to his ear. "But not what you wanted."

"It wasn't my decision to make."

The way she was deliberately not answering was as telling as if she had. He decided a different tack was called for. "You know," he said carefully, "if you're not comfortable working for us, you might be happier elsewhere."

She bristled, her spine going ramrod straight. "This is my home."

"I understand that. And I believe we made it clear when we came here that we'd like to be able to keep everyone on so you can remain here. But we can't have people working for us we can't trust. This business is too important to both Meredith and me. I hope you understand that."

"Of course," she said stiffly.

"Good. Now, is there anything else you think Meredith and I should know about Sutton Hall that we don't already?"

Grace paused for a brief moment as though seriously considering it, then finally said, "I don't believe so."

Did that mean there really wasn't anything they should know, or that Grace didn't think they should know anything else? Still not in the mood to trust the woman, Adam wasn't sure which possibility he was more inclined to believe.

Even so, from the woman's body language he doubted pressing her would result in getting anything else from her at the moment. He'd have to be satisfied for now—and keep a closer eye on her.

"All right," he said. "That will be all, then. Thank you, Grace."

With a tight nod, she pivoted on her heel and strode to the door.

When she was almost there, he called out. "Grace?"

She glanced back, a noticeable hint of nervousness on her face.

"Do you know why the passageways are there?"

"I believe they were intended to be used by the servants, to allow them to bring up food quickly from the kitchen without having to travel through the whole house."

That made sense given their location, Adam admitted. The rooms in the towers and the ones directly next to them were the biggest in the house and the most likely to be occupied by important people in the household, who would require the best service. With the kitchen near the center of the ground floor, a servant could easily pass through the servants' hallways down there and up through the towers.

"And who else knows about the passages?"

"The rest of the staff, I believe."

And not one of them thought to tell him and Meredith. Maybe they'd assumed that it was Grace's job to do so and that she would, or maybe they'd simply been following her lead in keeping them secret. Either way, Adam didn't think it said much about their loyalty to him and Meredith.

"Thank you."

When the door closed behind her, Adam glanced at Meredith, who hadn't said a word during the meeting. "Do you think I was too hard on her?"

"No," she said with a slight shake of her head. "She should have told us. You have to wonder what else she's keeping from us."

"Exactly what I was thinking," he said. "Do you think we should fire her?"

"I'd hate to. Like she said, this is her home. She's been here for so long. I don't know where she'd go."

"For all we know she has a million bucks stashed away and a thousand relatives she can go to."

"Just another indication of how little we know her."

"The question is, what should we do about the tunnels? I'm not really comfortable knowing there's a series of passages within the house that allow people access to so much of the house and apparently some of the rooms. At the very least, it could pose an issue for guest safety."

The color drained from her face. "You think Jillian won't want to stay?"

Adam grimaced. "No, I think she doesn't intend to go anywhere. I'm more concerned with her wandering around in the walls and having the run of the place."

"You're right. That's probably not a good idea. It might not be safe."

For more than one reason, Adam thought. Besides the obvious risk that she might be injured, he still didn't trust why she'd gone searching for those tunnels in the first place or why she was so determined to explore them. The woman was up to something, and whatever it was he doubted it would be good for them.

Before he and Grace had left the kitchen to find Meredith, he'd casually suggested to Rosie and Jillian that it might be a good time for them to go over the wedding menu. As expected, Rosie had jumped at the idea. He hadn't missed the irritated look Jillian had shot him, making it clear she hadn't liked being saddled with a babysitter. He'd almost pointed out that she should be happy talking about the menus, since they were for her wedding. He would have enjoyed getting her response to that.

But the fact of the matter was, he couldn't expect to keep her occupied and chaperoned the whole time she was here.

This could be exactly what he needed to force her to leave.

Except, as he'd said, he didn't believe for a second she'd go that easily.

"Now, CHICKEN IS always a good choice for an entrée," Rosie declared. "It's popular, just about anybody can eat it and there are so many ways I can prepare it...."

Seated at the kitchen island, Jillian fought her impatience with the situation—and her irritation with the man who'd put her in it. She hadn't missed the small, smug smile Adam had tossed her as Rosie effectively trapped her in the kitchen to go over the wedding menu. Just the thought of it—and him—brought back the frown she was trying to resist showing.

The man was diabolical.

She didn't have time for this. She needed to get out of here.

Not really listening as Rosie went on, she waited for her first chance to escape. The only other thing standing in her way was Ed. He sat on the other side of the island, slowly drinking a cup of coffee, giving no indication he was paying any attention to her or listening to anything his wife said.

Jillian studied him out of the corner of her eye. His head was bowed slightly, a small smile on his lips, his gaze focused on the counter in front of him, as though his thoughts were far away. Once again, she tried to get a sense of what the man was thinking, but his expression was as carefully guarded as everyone else's around here.

"On the other hand, I do know where I can get some good quality beef if that's more what you have in mind...."

Rosie stepped into the pantry adjoining the kitchen, the rest of her comment drifting out into the room as she kept talking.

This was her chance. Jillian shot a glance at Ed.

And met his eyes.

She realized with a jolt he hadn't been as un-involved as he'd appeared. He'd been waiting for Rosie to step out, too.

The smile on his face was friendly, pleasant. She saw immediately it didn't reach his eyes. They were much more direct, almost pointed.

He jerked his head slightly to the left. "Door's right over there," he said mildly, almost under his breath, indicating the one that led outside.

She wondered briefly why he was helping her escape his wife. Rosie wouldn't be happy Jillian was gone, and she seemed to have no trouble taking out her irritations on her husband. He was probably going to be berated as soon as Rosie found her missing.

Whatever the reason, she wasn't going to turn down the help, especially not when Rosie could come out of the pantry at any moment. "Thank you," she murmured, quickly rising to her feet.

He didn't respond, simply lowering his eyes and lifting his cup to his lips.

Without a glance back, Jillian hurried to the side door and ducked outside.

She did so without an ounce of regret. She didn't have time to deal with her pretend wedding. She had more important things to think about.

Quickly moving along the side of the house, she drew in a breath. It felt good to be outside after wandering around in the walls, and the fresh air might be just what she needed to clear her head and think.

Now that she knew about the passageway, it just left the question of who had actually used it last night to attack her. Grace had obviously known about it, and Jillian had to believe the rest of the staff did as well. Any one of them could have used it. At least, any one of them with access to the house, she amended. She wondered briefly if that meant she could eliminate Ray and Zack. Unlike Grace, Rosie and Ed, they didn't live within Sutton Hall. Then again, she wouldn't be surprised if Ray or Zack had keys to the main house, or knew an alternate way in, which meant they were still as viable as suspects as anyone.

Noticing she'd nearly reached the gardens, she turned and studied the lush greenery up ahead. They weren't far from the side door to the kitchen; she could have taken this route yesterday when she'd wanted to see the tower. Which meant that if Ray or Zack did have a key, it wouldn't have been much trouble for either of them to get from the groundskeeper's cottage to the kitchen and up to her room.

She was standing there, considering the possibilities, when the sound of approaching footsteps reached her. She looked up just in time to see Ray coming around the corner. He came to an abrupt stop as soon as he saw her, his expression quickly souring.

As if realizing at the last moment that he had to be polite, he managed to work up a thoroughly unconvincing smile and nodded. "Afternoon."

"Hi there."

Apparently satisfied the formalities had been dispensed with, he lowered his head and walked around her, continuing on his way.

She quickly moved to follow him, not about to lose this chance to talk to him. "It's a beautiful day out."

"Enjoy it while you can. Supposed to be a storm coming in tomorrow."

"I noticed you don't live in the house like Grace and the Warrens. Do you have your own quarters?"

"There's a groundkeeper's cottage out back."

"Is that where you raised Zack?"

"Yep."

"Zack mentioned his mother took off when he was a child."

"The boy talks too much," he muttered.

"That must have been very hard on you."

"It wasn't the most fun day of my life, but we got by."

"Did you ever hear from her again?"

"Nope. And good riddance."

"That didn't worry you?"

He snorted. "No. Why would it?"

"Something could have happened to her. She might not even be alive anymore."

"Not my concern."

She frowned at the coldness in his voice. "She's still the woman you married, still Zack's mother."

He came to an abrupt halt and whirled to face her. "And she didn't want to be either one. Some women aren't cut out to be a wife or a mother. I only wish she would have figured that out beforehand and saved us all the trouble."

She stared at him, fighting a shudder at the utter coldness on his face. "I—I'm sorry."

"You ask a lot of questions."

Jillian mustered a smile. "I'm curious about people."

"No offense, ma'am, but you can go be curious somewhere else. I have work to do."

With that, he put his back to her and continued down the path, quickly vanishing behind the greenery. Jillian didn't bother to try to follow him. She figured she'd gotten as much out of him as she was going to, and probably far more than she had any right to expect.

Considering his words, she made her way back to the entrance to the garden.

Her head lowered in thought, she was nearly to the front of the house when she spotted something blocking the path in front of her. She jerked her head up.

Adam stood a few feet away, watching her. At the sight of him, the sunlight shining down upon him, her heart jumped. Out of surprise, she told herself, unwilling to admit it was from anything else. Like how good he looked in the sunlight.

The sunlight that still couldn't illuminate the darkness in his eyes.

"I've been looking for you," he said.

She held her hands out, palms toward him. "Well, here I am."

His eyes narrowed with suspicion. "What are you doing out here?"

"After wandering around in those tunnels I figured I could use the fresh air."

The way his lips thinned, Jillian knew he didn't exactly believe her. "That's actually why I was looking for you," he said, his tone sending a prickle of warning down her spine. "Could I see you in my office?"

THEY DIDN'T SPEAK as they made their way back into the house.

When they arrived back at his study, Adam held the door for Jillian to enter first before following her inside. As soon as the door was closed behind him, he strode past her toward the desk.

"What's this about?" she asked.

Adam stopped behind the desk and turned to face her. "Given this recent…discovery, I'm not sure we can allow you to stay here any longer."

She hadn't moved closer, still standing near the door. She simply looked at him, as though not understanding. "Why not?"

"I don't know how extensive the passages are or what condition they're in, and frankly, I can't trust that you'll stay out of them."

"We were both in them and they were perfectly fine."

"You can't know that for sure. We couldn't really see much with your flashlight. And even if they were perfectly fine, you still managed to fall."

"It was a little stumble. It could have happened anywhere." She held up a hand when he would have interrupted. "But if it would make you more comfortable, what if I agree to stay out of the passageways?"

He almost laughed. "Like I said, I don't think I can trust you. To stay out of them," he added, almost as an afterthought.

From her narrowed eyes, she hadn't missed that little pause.

"Alternately…"

Jillian immediately perked up, exactly as he'd known she would.

Adam picked up a piece of paper. Glancing

at it, he grimaced, then slid it across the desk to her. "You can sign this waiver releasing us from any liability in case of injury."

Eyeing him closely, she slowly edged to the desk and took the paper from him.

"Are you expecting something to happen to me?"

"Are you so sure it won't?"

"Like I told you, I can take care of myself. Unless there's a reason you don't think I can..."

He nearly shook his head. She was impossible. "It wouldn't be responsible of me not to consider any possible consequences."

She stared at him for a long moment, and he wondered if she might actually decline to sign the document, felt a flicker of hope that this might be what got her to leave.

Lowering the paper to the desktop, she picked up the pen beside it and signed on the designated line.

Damn it.

Before she could pull her hand away, he reached out and caught her arm, holding her in place. Her eyes flew to his.

"It's really that important for you to be here?" he demanded.

"Yes, it is," she said seriously, her gaze as steely as he knew his own had to be. Then she slowly smiled, forcing a lightness in her tone and expression that didn't quite reach her eyes. "I want the wedding of my dreams."

Damn her. He didn't know what game she was playing, but it was clear she intended to play it out to the end. He just wasn't sure what the end would be, more convinced than ever it would be a bad one. For all of them.

Yet knowing that didn't get him to release her from his hold. Didn't keep him from noticing just how soft her skin was, or how fast her pulse was racing beneath his fingertips. Even as he registered it, he felt it kick up another notch, throbbing insistently under his touch. Felt his own pick up speed in response, the heat of her skin seeming to sink into his own, entering his bloodstream and sending a straight shot of adrenaline to his heart.

Neither of them moved. He waited for her to resist, to try to pull away, to seem outraged, to prove that one of them was sane.

She didn't, remaining utterly still, simply staring back at him. He might have believed she was completely unaffected. Except he knew she wasn't. He held the evidence in his hands, her pulse still pounding unsteadily beneath his fingers.

Was this all part of her game?

The fact that he didn't know—and that it wasn't enough to kill his own foolish reaction— was reason enough to let her go.

He made himself relax his fingers and release her, even when all he wanted to do was pull her closer.

She took a single step back, letting her arm fall to her side.

"Is that all?" she said blandly.

"That's all."

With a slight nod, she turned her back to him. She walked to the door at an unhurried pace, as though nothing had happened, as though she hadn't been affected by the contact at all. He watched her every step of the way, unable to look away.

So he didn't miss it when, just before she slipped out the door, she reached out and touched the wrist he'd held with her opposite hand, rubbing lightly at the spot where his fingers had been.

A strange combination of victory and dread rose inside him. She hadn't been as immune to the moment as she wanted to pretend.

She's either engaged or a liar, he reminded himself.

And more than ever, he suddenly wasn't sure which he wanted her to be less.

THE SLUT WAS too clever for her own good. Somehow she'd managed to find the passages and ruin everything. They were no longer secret enough, no longer safe to use.

It wasn't going to be enough to save her.

All of this could have been avoided if she had died the way she was supposed to—a tragic, untimely death in her sleep.

Instead she lived. To continue planning her wedding, all the while panting after a man who wasn't her husband-to-be. Wandering alone with him in those very passages. Going to his office for private meetings.

When she'd come out she'd been flushed, her face dark red, a small, slight smile on her lips. Agitated. Excited.

Aroused?

Disgusting.

She had to be stopped. And she would be.

Soon.

Chapter Ten

It was raining when Jillian woke the next morning. It took her a moment to recognize the sound when she opened her eyes. It wasn't the light patter of raindrops on the windows. No, it was the roaring of a torrential downpour, the wind howling, the rain coming down in sheets strong enough to batter the glass.

She turned her head toward the window to see it was still ominously dark outside, the sky a thick, impenetrable gray. She almost would have found it easier to believe it was still the middle of the night. Only the fact that it wasn't completely black out gave any sign it wasn't.

Just another day at Sutton Hall, she thought, grimacing. She could only imagine how gloomy the manor would be in the rain.

Turning her head in the other direction, she spotted the chair she'd leaned against the passageway door, where it would have been knocked over if the passage was opened. It had seemed unlikely the attacker would return. By dinner it had been common knowledge that she and the Suttons knew about the passages, leading to some unspoken tension between the Suttons and the staff. The attacker would have to be crazy to try to use it again to enter her room knowing she was aware of it.

Except, of course, it was pretty clear that "crazy" was exactly what this person was.

But the night had passed without incident. She hadn't heard a sound, the chair was still standing and the passageway remained closed.

And the threat remained, still lurking somewhere in the manor, no doubt waiting for a chance to strike again.

Shoving aside the sense of foreboding, Jillian showered and dressed, then made her way down to the kitchen. As usual, Rosie was at her station behind the counter, bustling about, preparing breakfast. But beneath her usual industriousness, Jillian sensed she was more agitated than usual, her body rigid with tension, her face heavy with a frown.

"Good morning," Jillian said tentatively.

Rosie glanced up and nodded before returning her attention to what she was doing. "Morning. Breakfast is almost ready. I'll get you set up in the dining room right quick."

"That's all right. I don't mind eating in here."

Sitting alone in the dining room at that massive table didn't sound like much fun at the moment.

Rosie opened her mouth as though prepared to argue, then simply shook her head. "Suit yourself. Have a seat."

Jillian eased herself into a chair at the kitchen table. "It looks pretty bad outside."

"That it does," Rosie agreed. "Supposed to get even worse by tonight."

"Do you get a lot of storms like this around here?"

"Sometimes. Up here in the mountains, never know how bad it'll get, with the wind and all. This one's supposed to be worse than most, though."

Jillian figured that explained the woman's mood. She couldn't blame her, as she took in the rain lashing the windows only a few feet away. It looked even darker outside from this vantage point. If it was this bad already, she didn't want to imagine how much worse it could get by nightfall.

"It rained on my wedding day," Rosie murmured. Jillian glanced over at her in surprise. The woman's eyes were focused on the windows, her gaze far away. "I probably should have considered that some kind of omen."

"What do you mean?" Jillian asked, curious. The woman didn't respond at first. After a moment, she suddenly blinked and shook herself, as though only just realizing she'd spoken aloud. Pressing her lips together, Rosie gave her head a slight shake and went back to cooking.

Any hope Jillian had of getting Rosie to open up a little more was quickly dashed. Rosie was in no mood to talk, deflecting Jillian's attempts with a few brusque words and going about her business. Jillian was left to eat in silence and contemplate the gathering storm.

Jillian was almost finished with breakfast when the door to the dining room suddenly swung open and Grace stepped through. Scanning the room, she finally spotted Jillian and smiled. "Good morning, Ms. Jones. I was just looking for you. Ms. Sutton asked me to show you to the ballroom. She said you were interested in seeing it and she has some ideas to show you."

Jillian knew there was a ballroom, of course, having seen pictures on the website. It hadn't been fully restored yet, but those glimpses had made it clear it was a beautiful space and Jillian had been eager to see it in person. But the idea of venturing anywhere alone with Grace was much less appealing.

Jillian eyed the woman carefully, trying to keep the wariness off her face. Grace was as impossible to read as ever, something Jillian was starting to find more and more unnerving. Jillian suspected Grace wasn't the only one who'd known about the passageways. Chances were everyone at Sutton Hall who'd worked here for years had. But Grace was the only one who'd known for sure, and who'd lied about it, and Jillian couldn't help but view her with extra suspicion.

Not that she could afford to show it, of course. She mustered a smile. "That sounds great. Thanks." There was no way to decline the offer, and no plausible reason she could. If anything, this might give her a chance to crack the woman.

"Thank you for breakfast, Rosie," Jillian said. She started to rise from the table, picking up her plate as she did.

"Leave it," Rosie ordered, gesturing toward the plate. "I'll get it." She glanced back at the windows, her gaze far away as she took in the rain, as though she'd already forgotten Jillian was there.

Doing as Rosie had asked, Jillian followed Grace out of the kitchen, through the dining room and back out into the main hall.

The ballroom was on the second floor in the west wing. Jillian fell into step beside Grace as she led the way up the staircase. She could imagine partygoers in all their finery making this very walk, through the entryway, up the curving staircase and on to the ballroom.

"I'm sorry about yesterday. With the tunnels," Jillian added when Grace shot her a look. "I hope I didn't get you into trouble."

"It's my own fault. I should have realized that with so many new people here now it would be impossible to keep some things private."

Jillian couldn't help but wonder if Grace had more in mind than just the tunnels when talking about things she'd wanted to keep private. "You didn't think even the Suttons needed to know about them?"

"It truly never occurred to me to tell them before. I'd all but forgotten about the passage-ways. No one's used them in years. They were hardly needed when Mr. Sutton was alive and there were only four of us living here."

Jillian honestly couldn't tell if she believed her. Before she could decide, they'd reached the second floor. Grace didn't slow for an instant, immediately moving down the corridor.

"After all those years of it just being the four of you, it must be strange for you having people like me coming in and being given the run of the place." Out of the corner of her eye, Jillian carefully watched Grace's reaction to the subject.

There was none. Not a single muscle moved on her face. "Sutton Hall is a magnificent build-ing," she said. "It really should be shared with people. It deserves to be better known."

"You really do love this place."

Grace nodded. "I do," she said dispassionately.

"You must have been relieved the Suttons decided to keep you on."

For the first time, a trace of emotion cracked the woman's cool facade, the flash so brief Jillian wasn't sure what it was. Irritation? Anger? Pain? "Yes. This has been my home for so long I can't imagine where else I could go. Mr. and Ms. Sutton have been quite generous to allow me to stay."

"But that doesn't make it any easier having new people come in and take over a house that feels more like yours than theirs, does it?"

"No, I suppose it doesn't." She smiled slightly, with a trace of sadness. It was the first genuine emotion Jillian could remember seeing from the woman, and made her seem much more human. In an instant, Jillian's perspective shifted and it was as if she was seeing Grace with new eyes. Outwardly the woman projected cool competence, but beneath that chilly exterior was a real woman with a deep well of sadness.

Even as Jillian felt a twinge of sympathy, the sad smile began to fade, the woman's mask falling back into place. "Things change, and not everything works out the way we like. And we all have no choice but to adjust to that. I suppose the biggest mistake one can make is to try to hold on to something that can't be kept."

Before Jillian could decide how to interpret that, they stopped in front of a set of double doors. Jillian noticed one of them was already ajar.

As if realizing she'd confessed more than she'd intended to, Grace gave her head a small shake and straightened her spine. She gestured to the door. "Here we are. I'm sure Ms. Sutton will be along shortly, if she's not inside already."

"You're not coming in?"

"I'm afraid I have some tasks to tend to before the storm gets worse." She frowned slightly. "Unless you'd like me to…?"

"No," Jillian said automatically with a wave of her hand. "That's not necessary. Thank you for bringing me up here."

"Of course." With a nod, Grace turned and started back down the hallway.

Jillian pushed the door open all the way and peered inside. Before her was a massive, cavernous space. There were a few dim lights turned on, but they didn't come close to illuminating the entire area. Long shadows stretched across the floor, and she couldn't even get a sense how big it truly was.

It suddenly struck her that being alone here might not be a good idea. She glanced back, only to find Grace already halfway down the corridor and rapidly vanishing from view. There was no way to call her back without it looking odd.

Ten minutes ago she hadn't been sure she wanted to be alone with Grace—now she wasn't sure she wanted to be alone without her. *Make up your mind,* she told herself.

Taking a breath, she poked her head through the doorway and surveyed the space. One glance was all it took to take her breath away.

The room was massive, standing two stories high and stretching as far in length. Along the walls were huge mirrors that reflected the space back in on it. The ceiling was dotted with elaborate crystal chandeliers, and right in the middle of it was a domed skylight revealing the heavens. She could imagine the view it must offer on a clear evening, the starlight sparkling through the glass. At the moment all that could be seen were the churning gray clouds of the storm outside.

It would certainly be an impressive space for a wedding reception, or one of the balls it had been intended for over a century ago. As she stepped onto the hardwood floor, her footsteps echoing high into the ceilings far overhead, it was almost as if she could sense the ghosts of long-forgotten dancers moving around her, still taking their turns on the floor.

There was a stage on one side, closed off by

heavy curtains. If Meredith was here, she could be back there.

Jillian called out. "Hello?"

The only response was her own voice echoing back at her, repeating several times, each one softer, until it was barely a whisper.

The sound only emphasized the emptiness of the space—and just how alone she was in it.

Unease flickered along her nerve endings, raising goose bumps on her skin. She remembered her earlier instinct, that she shouldn't be in here alone. She'd let her curiosity override her common sense. There was no telling what—or who—could be lurking in the murky shadows. She should wait outside, in the relative safety of the hall.

She started to turn back to the door—

It burst open, a large figure filling the frame, looming in front of her.

She nearly screamed, her heart leaping into her throat, cutting off the sound and her breath.

Seconds later, Ray stepped over the threshold and into the room.

Before she could make a sound, his eyes met hers. He straightened in surprise. "What are you doing in here?"

Both his surprise and his irritation seemed genuine enough that she relaxed the tiniest bit.

He hadn't been expecting to find her here, hadn't seen her.

Hadn't been trying to scare her.

"I'm looking for Meredith," she explained, suddenly feeling foolish. "Have you seen her?"

He gave his head a sharp shake. "No." With that, he started into the room, brushing past her.

"What brings you here?" she asked.

"We need to get these windows covered. The storm's supposed to get pretty bad."

"Ed isn't taking care of it?" she asked, half wondering why the groundskeeper would be doing it.

"We're all pitching in. It's a big place. There's a lot to be done."

Before she could wonder who else he meant, Zack stepped through the doorway, carrying some wooden boards tucked under his arm. As soon as he spotted her, his lips curved in a smile. "Well, hey there."

Jillian resisted the eye roll that was becoming second nature when she encountered the man. "Good morning."

"Zack," Ray barked before his son could respond. "You can get started over there."

His jaw clenching, Zack nodded tightly and started toward where his father had indicated, though not before shooting Jillian a wink.

"Have you seen Meredith?" she asked him.

He called back over his shoulder. "Nope."

Frowning, she glanced back toward the open doorway. She wondered where Meredith was. In any case, Jillian would probably be better off looking for her elsewhere. She was only in the way here.

She looked around for Ray and Zack to ask them to tell Meredith she'd gone back downstairs, but didn't see either man. They seemed to have disappeared. The cavernous space before her was empty and still.

The goose bumps prickling again, she frowned and made her way back to the doorway.

She slipped into the hallway, relaxing slightly when she was back in the well-lit corridor. She glanced down it in both directions. It was empty. Meredith was nowhere in sight.

Jillian slowly made her way back to the main stairs, fully expecting Meredith to appear at any moment. As she did, she thought back to her conversation with Grace. The woman had said all the right things, but was she truly grateful to the Suttons for keeping her on? It would only be natural that she'd feel some resentment that she had to rely on their kindness at all. Despite what the woman had said, Jillian still wasn't convinced Grace was all that happy having anyone here, let alone new owners she had to report to.

She was still considering the question when

she reached the stairs. Preoccupied, she placed one hand on the railing.

It had barely made contact when she felt a sudden rush of motion behind her.

She didn't get a chance to process it, to turn toward the sound.

A split second later something crashed into her back and sent her flying forward.

A startled scream—short, shrill—tore from her mouth before her throat suddenly seized up in panic, in terror, cutting off the sound. She was launched in midair, and for an endless moment she could see the stairs stretching out below her, the bottom impossibly far away.

And then she was hurtling, plunging, tumbling downward. There wasn't even time to throw her hands out to try to soften her landing. Before she could raise her arms, the stairs were rushing up to meet her. She crashed hard on her right side, pain bursting in her shoulder and arm. Another scream pressed against her throat. It was cut off by the force of another blow as she continued to roll, her legs flying over her head and banging against the stairs. Explosions of pain erupted in her back, her hip, her arms and legs as she plunged down the stairs, different parts of her body striking the hard stone and sharp edges over and over again.

Finally, blessedly, she tumbled over one last

time, crashing onto her back on the landing, every inch of her body screaming in pain.

She lay there unmoving, trying to pull in a breath, to deal with the pain, to process what had just happened.

Pushed, she recognized faintly. Someone had pushed her down the stairs.

That was what the feeling of force against her back had been. There'd been no cry of warning, no sound of shock after the impact, nothing to indicate this had been an accident.

No. It had been deliberate. Someone had purposely shoved her down the stairs.

Staring blindly above her, she saw something enter her range of vision. Something at the top of the stairs.

Blinking rapidly, she tried to focus on the object, to see what it was.

It was a person, she registered, her heart pounding harder. The person who'd pushed her?

The figure gradually took form, the face becoming clearer, revealing—

Meredith, Jillian realized. The breath caught in her throat, surprise and confusion and wariness churning inside her.

Meredith stood at the top of the stairs. She made no sound, made no move to come down. She simply stood there, staring down at her.

Jillian peered closer, willing her eyes to focus, desperately trying to read the woman's face.

But no matter how hard Jillian tried, she couldn't read Meredith's expression, couldn't tell if she was peering down at her with shock that she'd fallen—or disappointment that it hadn't been so much worse....

Chapter Eleven

"Oh, my God."

Her attention fixed on the woman at the top of the stairs, Jillian heard the voice as though from a great distance. She vaguely recognized it as a man's, ragged with shock and concern.

And then Adam was there, leaning over her, cutting Meredith off from view.

"Jillian, are you all right?"

Still dazed, she had to force her mind to focus on the question. Was she all right? "I—I'm not sure. I think so."

"What happened?"

Someone pushed me down the stairs.

Jillian swallowed hard, trying to think of what to say, not sure how much she should reveal, especially when the person she suspected was—

"She must have fallen down the stairs."

Meredith, Jillian registered, her gut tightening with fresh suspicion. It was Meredith who answered, her voice rapidly coming closer. Jillian heard footsteps approaching quickly on the stairs.

Meredith, who'd been standing there, looking down at her.

Meredith, who'd pushed her?

"Did you see it happen?" Adam asked his sister without looking at her.

"No. I just heard the noise, and when I got to the top of the stairs, I saw her at the bottom."

Jillian couldn't see the woman with Adam in front of her. She wished she could, wished she had a chance to try to read her expression up close. It was impossible to tell anything from her voice. Meredith sounded believably horrified.

Grimacing, Adam nodded tightly and refocused on Jillian. "How do you feel? Are you in pain? Do you need me to call a doctor?"

The words drew her focus back to him. And in spite of the terror that had gripped her only moments earlier and the suspicion still racing through her mind, she felt heat rush through her at the open concern in his voice. His dark eyes, his chiseled features, usually so cold and remote, were softened with worry. For her.

It was the nicest he'd ever sounded when speaking to her, she realized with a flicker of amusement. If this was what it took, maybe she should have gotten shoved down the stairs long ago.

As she watched, the concern on his face deepened, and he went pale. "Meredith, call 911. I think she might have a concussion...."

Jillian flinched, and she realized she hadn't answered him, had simply been staring helplessly into his eyes. No wonder he thought she had a concussion.

"No, really, it's not that bad." She started to push herself up on her elbows. "I'm pretty sure nothing's broken." She flexed her legs and feet tentatively to test the statement. There was definite soreness, but no real pain to indicate any serious damage.

"Still, we should be careful. Let's get you back to your room and we'll see how bad it is."

Before she could protest, he swept her into his arms in one smooth motion as though she weighed nothing at all. She fell against his chest, the wall of his torso hard and solid as stone against her body. The arms around her were strong yet gentle, holding her close with the lightest of touches. She drew in a breath at the sudden surprise of his nearness, only to pull in the scent of him so deeply it seemed to fill all her senses. She almost felt light-headed from it.

Rising to his feet, he turned and began to quickly climb the stairs. She knew she should protest, tell him this wasn't necessary, that she was capable of walking. Instead, she found her head falling back against his shoulder instinctively, fitting as naturally as if it belonged there. Her eyes drifted shut almost automatically, as the feeling of being in his arms, surrounded by him, sank in. The past few days had been so hard. Having to keep on her guard, having to tell so many lies and not being able to trust anyone. For the first time since she'd arrived here, it was possible to forget all of that, if only for a moment. Who she was. Who he was. She sank into the feeling of being held against him, the safety in his arms. At that moment, nothing else existed in the world.

He suddenly slowed, and she knew before she opened her eyes that they'd arrived at her bedroom. He leaned forward and opened the door with one hand, the movement so careful she was barely jostled.

Moments later, he was lowering her onto the mattress. Once she was sitting upright, propped up against the pillows, he eased his arms out from under her.

To her surprise, he didn't move away immediately. Instead, he slid onto the edge of the bed and sat facing her. He peered at her closely, clearly looking for any signs of injury. "Are you sure you're all right? I think I'd feel better if we at least had you checked out by a doctor."

She gave her head a vigorous shake. "Really, I'm fine. A little sore, but thankfully no worse than that." Given some of the twinges she was feeling, she wouldn't be surprised if she had some bruises the next day. She figured she was better off not mentioning that. She didn't want him to use any injuries as an excuse to make her leave, and she wasn't going anywhere. Not without answers, especially after this.

"Can I at least get you something?" another voice asked.

Meredith stood near the door, her body rigid with tension.

Jillian studied her carefully. It was the first chance she'd had to do it since her fall, since she'd spotted the woman looking down at her, her expression unreadable.

Meredith clasped her hands in front of herself, gripping them so tightly her knuckles were white. Jillian wouldn't have been surprised if she started wringing them. Was it the woman's usual nervousness, or something more? Jillian simply couldn't tell, and she choked back a frustrated groan.

"Maybe some pain relievers?" Meredith suggested when Jillian didn't say anything.

Jillian did have some in her bag and wouldn't have minded taking a few at the moment, but wasn't about to admit it. "I'm fine," she said again.

"How about some tea?" Meredith murmured.

Jillian almost told her it wasn't necessary, but she suddenly wasn't sure how comfortable she was around the woman, either, not with so many questions whispering through her mind. "That would be nice."

"I'll have Rosie send some up." With a tight nod, Meredith turned and hurried from the room.

If Adam noticed anything strange about Meredith's behavior, he didn't show it. He turned his attention back to Jillian. "Are you sure I can't talk you into seeing that doctor?"

"I'm sure," she said firmly. "It's really not that bad."

She braced herself for his response, not expecting him to let her off the hook that easily.

He still managed to surprise her. He reached out and gently took her arm, lifting it from her lap and pulling it toward him.

His hands were warm against her skin, his fingers long and lean. He turned her arm over lightly, looking closely at her skin as though examining it for any signs of cuts or bruises. "How does that feel?" he murmured.

"Fine," she said, her voice sounding breathless to her ears.

He suddenly stopped, as though finally realizing how intimately he was touching her, and raised his head to meet her eyes.

Still he didn't let her go, his hold on her wrist gentle but unmistakable.

"You're sure?"

"Yes."

Finally, slowly, he lowered her arm to the bed. It didn't matter. She still undeniably felt his touch on her skin. "You gave us a real scare there," he said.

"Sorry about that."

"So what happened? Did you trip on the carpet? Were you not paying attention to where you were walking? Damn it, you have to be careful—"

She cut him off. "I didn't fall. I was pushed."

Adam didn't respond at first, simply staring at her in disbelief. "What are you talking about?"

"Before I went down the stairs, I felt hands on my back, felt someone shove me hard. I was pushed."

"That's absurd. Why would someone do that?"

"I don't know. You'd have to ask them."

"All right," he said, his tone an annoying mix of patient and patronizing. "Did you see anyone?"

Jillian hesitated for a second, unsure whether she wanted to admit what she'd seen or deal with the conflict that would inevitably arise. At the same time, she was curious what his reaction would be.

Pushing her misgivings away, she plowed forward. "After I fell, when I looked up I did see someone standing at the top of the stairs."

"Who?"

"Meredith."

He went completely still, his expression going blank. "What exactly are you suggesting?"

"I don't know exactly," she hedged, reading his face as closely as possible for any hint of what he was thinking. But his eyes remained as guarded as ever, his features revealing nothing. "Only that I know I was pushed, and Meredith was at the top of the stairs."

"You're saying you think Meredith pushed you," he said, his voice thick with accusation.

"Why would she do that?" she asked carefully, turning his question back on him.

"She wouldn't," he shot back. "If she had, she certainly wouldn't have stood there watching you fall."

She might if she wanted to make sure I didn't get up again, Jillian thought, biting her tongue to keep from saying it aloud.

"She clearly heard you scream and came to see what happened," he continued.

"I guess that makes sense," Jillian said softly, not sure what to believe. It was possible. But was it the truth?

Adam obviously didn't miss the halfheartedness of her agreement. His face darkening, he abruptly pushed away from her, rising to his feet. He stood glaring down at her, his expression rigid with controlled anger. "If you really believe someone pushed you down the stairs, then I'm sure you'll be wanting to leave as soon as possible. No reason to stay where someone means you harm, or to bring your wedding guests to such a place."

"Is that what you want?"

"I told you, what I want is for Meredith not to be hurt, and you seem determined to do just that."

"I'm only telling you what happened."

"Really? Because it sounds like you're making an accusation. If that's the case, I'm not interested. You can say anything you want about me, but don't ever say a word about my sister."

She stared at him, torn between admiration of his loyalty to his family and suspicion of what it meant. Meredith was an adult. Why was he so protective of her? What was he hiding?

She was still contemplating the question an instant later when he turned on his heel and strode toward the door.

Another figure was standing there, she immediately noticed. Ed filled the doorway, holding a tray in his hands, his usual smile nowhere in sight. His eyes shifted between her and Adam. She wondered how much he'd heard.

Seemingly recognizing his boss's anger, he shuffled to the side just inside the door, allowing Adam to brush by him without a word.

"Is that for me?" Jillian asked.

"Meredith said to bring you tea, and Rosie thought you could use some food. Sounded like you might not be eating enough, getting dizzy and all."

Jillian fought the urge to frown. Is that what everyone was thinking—she'd simply fallen? She supposed it made sense if you didn't know any better, which she did.

She managed to muster a smile. "That's very kind of her. Thank you for bringing it."

She expected him to move forward and bring the tray to her. Instead, he continued standing there, eyeing her with an expression she couldn't quite read.

"Is something wrong?" she asked.

"Shouldn't talk bad about a man's sister," he said. "Family means everything."

"Of course it does," Jillian agreed cautiously. "Do you have a sister?"

He hesitated briefly. "I used to."

The admission seemed to spur some reaction inside him, because he suddenly dropped his eyes and started forward. Without looking at her, he moved to the bedside table and carefully set the tray on top of it, then turned and walked from the room.

Strange, Jillian thought, as she had so many times since she'd arrived at Sutton Hall. She half wondered where Ed's sister was now, only to dismiss the idea a moment later with a shake of her head.

Throwing her legs over the side of the bed, she rose to her feet, ignoring the twinges of pain in her legs as she made her way to the door. It wasn't Ed's sister she was interested in. It was Adam's. And it was long past time she got some answers.

JILLIAN FOUND MEREDITH in the dining room, sitting on one side of the massive table. She made for a lonely figure, dwarfed by the size of both the table and the room around her. She might as well have been the only person in the world.

She acted like it, too, not looking up when Jillian entered, her attention fixed on whatever she was writing on the paper in front of her. The pencil in her hand scratched across the paper in furious strokes, the noise the only sound in the room.

Jillian opened her mouth to announce her presence, only to ease it shut again. Curious what the woman was focused on so intently, Jillian moved closer, keeping her footsteps quiet on the floor's thin rugs.

She finally came close enough to see that Meredith wasn't writing. She was drawing. The half-formed image continued to develop before Jillian's eyes, as Meredith's pencil slid over the page, filling in details, shading in nuance.

It was a bride and groom, dancing together in the middle of a ballroom Jillian recognized as the one upstairs. In a few deft strokes, Meredith had managed to depict the space so that it was easily identifiable, though the room in the drawing was decorated for a party, not empty like the one upstairs. The couple was holding each other tightly, positioned so that only the bride's face was visible. Beaming, she tilted her head back, her eyes closed, her mouth open as though she was laughing. Jillian could almost feel it herself, feel the joy shining from the bride's face in the way Meredith had drawn it.

"Is this what you wanted to show me in the ballroom?"

Meredith started, her head shooting up. At the same time, her pencil slipped, scrawling a jagged line across the page. Jillian instantly felt a pang of regret at the sight of that dark, errant line marring the image. "I'm sorry. I didn't mean to startle you."

Meredith looked down at the drawing, and

Jillian saw her wince as she took it in. The line could be erased, but it would take part of the image with it. It would take some work to put it back the way it had been, if she even could.

"No, it's all right," Meredith said. "I tend to get lost in my head when I'm working on something. I should have heard you come in. But, yes, I wanted to show you a few ideas I had and I thought these might make it easier to visualize what I had in mind when you saw the ballroom. And then I forgot one I particularly liked and had to go back for it and…" She fluttered a hand helplessly.

And I fell down the stairs, Jillian finished for her. So it hadn't just been a ploy by Grace or Meredith to get her up there. Meredith had had a perfectly reasonable explanation, or at least an excuse for one.

If it was true, then Meredith likely wouldn't have been in the west wing when Jillian was pushed. She would have been in the east wing, where the bedrooms were. Jillian thought back to the moments after she'd fallen, when she'd come to a stop on the landing where the staircase split in two and seen Meredith at the top of the stairs. She'd thought Meredith had been at the top of the stairs to the west wing, where the person who'd pushed her would have been standing. Was it possible she'd gotten turned around in the fall and been looking up at the top of the stairs to the east wing instead without realizing it? It would also explain why Meredith hadn't seen who pushed her, if she hadn't done it herself.

Jillian tried to remember what the rest of the scene had looked like, where the railing had been—on the right or the left?—but she couldn't bring the image into focus. She'd been so dazed after the fall, the only thing she'd seen clearly was Meredith.

Not quite ready to dismiss her suspicions entirely, Jillian sank into the chair to Meredith's right. "You're really good," she noted, nodding toward the drawing.

Meredith automatically shook her head. "I don't know about that."

"Well, I do, and I'm not just saying that. You have a lot of talent."

Quickly moving to cover the drawing with a blank sheet of paper, Meredith smiled thinly. "Thank you."

"Have you done any drawing professionally, or considered exploring it?"

Meredith shook her head harder, more adamant this time. "Oh, no. I couldn't."

"Why not?"

The question seemed to pull her up short. "Um, my hand," Meredith said weakly. Jillian glanced down, finally noticing the woman was flexing her fingers. "I…broke it. The bones didn't heal quite right and it still hurts, especially when I try writing with it."

"But you can still draw?"

Meredith grimaced. "No, it hurts to draw for too long, but I can't seem to stop. No matter how much it hurts, I just have to keep doing it." She laughed faintly. "I'm pretty sure that's the definition of stupidity."

"Or passion," Jillian suggested. "It's in your bones so much you can't let it go."

"I guess that's a nicer way to think of it," Meredith said, a wistful note in the words. With a sigh, she flexed her hand again, drawing her fingers into her palm and slowly straightening them. Even as she did it, Jillian noticed it took her some effort to do so and the motion wasn't smooth.

Curious, Jillian automatically reached out to take Meredith's hand without thinking.

Meredith immediately flinched, jerking back with a force that threatened to knock her chair out from under her. Jillian froze. Meredith's whole body was tense, her eyes wide with fear, as though she was being attacked.

"I—I'm sorry," Meredith said, swallowing deeply. She placed her hands flat on the tabletop, and Jillian could see her arms still shook slightly. "You startled me."

And Jillian immediately understood, all the

pieces clicking into place. Meredith's skittish-
ness. The way she always held herself defen-
sively. Adam's protectiveness toward his sister.
It wasn't just about a wedding business or the
fact that a mysterious death had taken place and
threatened to derail what they'd worked for.

Someone had hurt this woman.

And not just once. As Jillian watched, Meredith's shoulders hunched inward slightly, as
though preparing to ward off a blow. The posture was instinctive, as ingrained in her bones
as the need to draw.

"How did you break your hand?" Jillian asked
quietly. She knew it was none of her business,
but couldn't stop the question from coming out,
couldn't keep from wanting to know.

Meredith swallowed hard, not meeting Jillian's
eyes, her gaze fixed on the tabletop. Jillian wondered if she was going to answer, and was about
to apologize when Meredith finally did.

"My husband…had a temper." She exhaled
sharply, the breath emerging almost as a humor-
less laugh. "And I couldn't seem to do anything
right, no matter how hard I tried."

The words only confirmed Jillian's suspicions.
Sympathy and a trace of guilt welled in her chest,
at what the woman had clearly been through and
how Jillian had misinterpreted her behavior. "I'm
sorry," she said, meaning it. "But I'm glad you're

not in that situation anymore. That must have taken a lot of strength."

Meredith smiled faintly. "It did, but not mine. Adam saved me, when I couldn't save myself. He feels guilty for not knowing anything was happening, for not doing anything sooner. Which is ridiculous, of course. The only person responsible for me is me. How could he be to blame for not saving me when I couldn't save myself?"

And there it was, everything she needed to know to unlock the mystery that was Adam Sutton.

Of course he would go along with his sister's dream to open this place for weddings. Of course he would give up his career to do that for her. Of course he would refuse to let anyone speak ill of her, or do anything to hurt her.

That was the man he was.

"You're lucky to have him," Jillian said softly.

"I know."

"I'm a little surprised you'd want to have anything to do with marriage and weddings after going through that."

"If anything, I think I needed it. The idea of seeing happy couples on one of the best days of their lives…I could use that. It would be nice to be reminded that love does exist and people can be happy, you know?" She finally raised her head and met Jillian's eyes. "Like you and Ryan."

This time it was pure guilt—sharp and painful—that struck squarely in Jillian's chest. She had absolutely no idea what to say.

"I'm sorry," Meredith said, misreading Jillian's silence. "You're here to plan your wedding. I'm sure this is the last thing you want to hear about. Not that you have anything to worry about. Even without having met him, I know your fiancé has to be a good man. I know you wouldn't pick anyone who didn't deserve you. You're too strong for that. You're going to be happy. I know it."

It was Jillian's turn to force a smile, her heart sinking at the kindness—the hope—shining in the woman's eyes. All of which was based on a lie.

Oh, God. When Meredith learned the truth she was going to be crushed.

The suspicious part of her, which couldn't forget what had happened to Courtney, and what had happened to Jillian herself over the past few days, prodded at the back of her brain, forcing her to consider the possibilities the new information raised. If anything, this might give Meredith some kind of twisted motive, leading her to take out the pain of what was done to her on other couples....

But looking into the woman's eyes, Jillian knew deep in her heart it couldn't possibly be true. There was too much kindness, too much hope, in her expression. She really did want to believe in that kind of happiness. She wouldn't do anything to destroy it.

Whatever had happened to Courtney, whoever had attacked Jillian, this woman wasn't responsible.

It meant she could trust Adam, Jillian realized, relief crashing over her. Knowing all of this put the man and his actions in a whole new light.

Of course it was possible he, too, might still have some unknown motive to go after women who were about to be married. But even if he did, she simply didn't believe he would do that here, under these circumstances. He never would have killed Courtney, never would have tried to do anything to her. He wouldn't have done that to Meredith. He knew how much this wedding business meant to her, and she meant too much to him.

Which meant, exactly as he'd told her from the beginning, he wasn't going to be happy about how Jillian had lied.

Neither would Meredith. But while her brother would be angry, it was Meredith's response Jillian suddenly dreaded more.

She needed to talk to Adam. She needed to tell him the truth.

She could start here, of course. Meredith was sitting right in front of her, still smiling at her.

Jillian couldn't bring herself to open her mouth. She was enough of a coward that she would rather face Adam Sutton's rage than break his sister's heart.

Chapter Twelve

Thunder rumbled outside, the sound vibrating the window at Adam's back. The storm was picking up.

The dismal weather perfectly matched his mood. Adam stared at the papers on the desk in front of him without seeing them. He needed to focus, but no matter how hard he tried, he couldn't.

No, he was doing exactly what he'd done for the past hour—stewing over Jillian Jones.

It was bad enough that he was attracted to a woman whom he didn't trust, whose motives for being here he didn't believe, or who, if she was telling the truth, might be engaged. But the idea she could be unhinged enough to think Meredith had pushed her down the stairs made the fact that he still couldn't get her out of his head even worse.

The way she'd felt in his arms. The way she'd looked lying on the bed, peering up at him from the pillows.

The way she'd looked accusing his sister of trying to hurt her.

Damn it.

He had to get her out of here. Now more than ever.

He was making another attempt at forcing the words in front of him to make sense when someone knocked on the door.

Thankful for the distraction, he glanced up from the desk. "Come in."

In the split second before the door opened, he realized it was her. Somehow he'd managed to become that ridiculously attuned to the woman in such a short amount of time.

As expected, she poked her head in, the sight of her face sending his pulse up a notch, then slid all the way inside, closing the door behind her back. Immediately the room seemed smaller, too confined. "I need to talk to you."

He rose from the desk. "All right. Why don't we go out—?"

"No," Jillian said, stepping forward as he rounded the desk to move for the door. "Here. I need to talk to you alone."

He stopped, eyeing the woman before him and the door behind her, which suddenly looked very far away. "I'm not sure that's such a good idea."

The corners of her mouth quirked slightly. "Am I that scary to be around?"

"I'm just not sure how appropriate it is."

The smile fading, she stopped a few feet away and squared her shoulders, looking directly into his eyes. "I'm not engaged. I'm not getting married. I never was. That's not why I'm here."

It took a few seconds for the words to register. He could only stare at her dumbly at first.

Then a thousand different emotions exploded inside him all at once. Disbelief. Anger. Triumph. Relief.

A sudden, ridiculous jolt of something that felt like...*joy*.

Anger. He'd go with anger. For doing this to Meredith. For wasting her time.

In a heartbeat, every inch of his body had tensed with barely contained fury. Damn it, he'd known it all along. It took everything he had not to yell. He managed to force out a tight, restrained "Get out."

"No," she said without blinking or moving a muscle. "Not until I get what I came for."

"And what the hell is that?"

"The truth. Courtney Miller was my best friend. I'm here to find out what happened to her."

He hadn't expected anything she said to stop him cold again, but once again he was struck dumb. *Oh, hell*. The anger weakened slightly as a twinge of sympathy struck. All right, so she was grief-stricken. He could somewhat understand the lies, even if he couldn't excuse them.

"Your friend died in a tragic accident—"

"No, she didn't," she said furiously, for the first time displaying an anger that rivaled his own. "Courtney was afraid of heights. She never would have been out on that balcony. It doesn't make any sense."

Seeing the emotion bursting from her almost tempered his fury toward her completely. Clearly she wasn't lying about her relationship to Courtney Miller. The woman had obviously meant a great deal to her. But that didn't change the facts.

He gentled his tone further. "I'm sorry, Jillian, but it's the only explanation that does make sense."

"No, it's not. Courtney was murdered."

He swallowed a sigh. "That's ridiculous—"

"Really? Are you going to try to convince me that all the things that have happened to me since I've gotten here didn't happen, either?"

"You mean falling down the stairs?" he said, unable to hold back his disbelief at the story she'd told him, her accusations toward Meredith.

"I was pushed," she said through gritted teeth.

"By Meredith?"

"No," she said. "I talked to her. She told me about…her marriage. Why this business means so much to her. I don't believe she'd jeopardize that. It wasn't her."

Any relief he might have felt at her withdrawal of that ridiculous accusation was overruled by fresh anger that she'd forced Meredith to talk about that bastard. "Then who?"

"The same person who tried to suffocate me in my sleep two nights ago. I fought them off, but they managed to get in and out of my room unnoticed. That's what made me decide to start looking for hidden passageways around here."

Adam frowned, doubt tempering the instinctive outrage that someone would do that to her. "Are you sure you weren't just dreaming?"

"I know I wasn't," she said firmly, her voice ringing with conviction.

"Why didn't you say something before?"

"I figured if I said someone attacked me in my room, you'd expect me to want to leave, and I didn't know how to explain that I wasn't going anywhere."

"Why not explain the truth about who you are and what you were doing here? If you're right, how long were you willing to put your life at risk before saying something?"

"As long as I had to. I didn't know if I could trust you, and I couldn't afford to have you make me leave, not before I knew the truth."

"Then why are you telling me now?"

"Because of what Meredith told me. I finally understand why you're here, why you decided to open Sutton Hall for weddings with Meredith. I don't believe you would do anything to jeopardize her dream. Which means you can't be responsible for any of this."

She'd thought *he* could be a killer? The idea stung, maybe more than it should considering he'd thought she was a liar.

"I could still make you leave." Was still *going* to.

"No, you won't."

With anyone else, he would have been amazed at the certainty in her voice in challenging him. With this woman, all he felt was a reluctant admiration at her audacity. He arched a brow. "Oh, really? And why not?"

"Because you have just as much reason to want to get to the truth as I do. You're right, there's someone here who can hurt Meredith, but it's not me. As long as there's someone on the loose at Sutton Hall who's this dangerous, Meredith's dream won't come true. And people have already been hurt. Someone murdered Courtney, and they've been targeting me since I've gotten here. There won't be any weddings at Sutton Hall, not as long as someone is attacking any bride who comes here."

"But why would somebody do that?"

"They obviously don't want anyone getting married here."

"For what reason? Everyone who works here needs this business to succeed to keep this place up and running or we'll probably have to sell."

"I don't know. That's what I'm trying to find out. It's what you should be trying to figure out. So help me. Let's work together."

"Assuming that you're right, I can try to solve this myself. I don't need you here, especially if you are right and someone has been attacking you."

"How will you explain to Meredith why I'm leaving? That she can't have any more weddings here? Or will you even bother? Would you let some other couple come here and put their lives at risk? Or are you hoping no one else will come?"

"What are you suggesting?" he challenged, even though he knew perfectly well. That didn't mean he liked it, or believed it for a second.

Didn't he? some small part of him asked.

"Let's set a trap. This person is already coming after me. Let's catch them in the act. Let's catch *them*."

He could only stare at her in astonishment, unable to believe what she was proposing. Then again, this was her. He could believe it all too well, and he knew without a doubt she meant every word. "You're out of your mind."

"No, I'm not."

"If you think I'm going to let you put yourself in danger like this, you are."

"I'm already in danger. I only want to use that to my advantage and catch this bastard."

"If you're right, then we're dealing with someone who's seriously deranged. You can't predict how someone like that will behave. You won't have an advantage."

"I've told you from the start I can take care of myself. You don't need to worry about me."

"Well, clearly someone needs to!"

"I don't need you to protect me. I'm not your sister!"

The idea was so ridiculous a laugh burst from his throat. "Trust me, I definitely don't think you're my sister."

"Then don't treat me like it!"

She threw the words out like a gauntlet, the challenge impossible to resist, tearing down the last bit of resistance to what he'd wanted to do for so long.

And there was only one thing he could do.

He surged forward, erasing that last, irrevocable step between them, and captured her face in his hands, taking her mouth with his.

IN THE LAST few seconds before he kissed her, before he touched her, before he erased what little distance remained between their bodies, Jillian felt no surprise. Deep down, she'd known it was coming, had been waiting for it. With every ounce of tension building from the pit of her stomach and gripping her body, with every bit of awareness racing along her nerve endings and electrifying her skin, she'd known. There was only one place this had been leading to, only one place it could possibly go.

And then, finally, amazingly, it happened.

He was right in front of her, no space separating them. His hands were cupping her face, pulling her toward him.

And his mouth was on hers.

He devoured her, his lips firm and hot and insistent as they worked against her own. Their mouths mashed together furiously, desperately, hungrily. Every stroke of his tongue, every brush of his lips, just made her want more. Of this. Of him. And from the way he met her every inch of the way, deepening the kiss second by second, she could tell he felt the same.

A giddy rush of delight spiraled through her. It seemed as if she'd been waiting to kiss this man forever, maybe from the first time she'd seen him coming down the main stairs. And now it was happening. Now his lips were on hers, his tongue sliding against her own, teasing and toying and tasting her. Now she knew what he felt like, tasted like. Her hands grabbed at his chest, for something to hold on to, to pull him close. She caught two fistfuls of his sweater and held him tighter to her, wanting every bit of him against her, needing him as near as he could possibly be.

He tore his mouth from hers just long enough to murmur, "This is crazy."

"I know."

He chuckled. His mouth back against hers, she felt it vibrate through him and into her. "My God, you're the most infuriating woman I've ever met in my entire life."

It was her turn to laugh. "You're not exactly an easy case yourself."

"Guilty."

Beneath her hands she could feel his heart pounding, feel the hardness of his chest, the heat radiating from him. And she instantly wanted more. Needed more. Needed to feel his hot skin against hers. Needed to feel his arms wrapped around her. Needed to feel his heart pounding against his chest, the insistent rhythm vibrating through his skin and into hers.

He suddenly pulled away, robbing her of that precious heat. "I have to ask—"

"What?" she demanded, staring at his mouth, wishing it was on her.

"The man in the pictures with you. Your 'fiancé.' Is he…?"

"Just a friend." A chuckle eased from her lungs. "And very gay."

He matched her laugh. "Good."

And then his mouth was back on hers.

They tore at each other's clothes, sweaters pulled over heads, pants released and shoved aside, her bra dispensed with, his boxers kicked off. And in between, they stole every touch they could. She ran her fingertips over his abs, his side, his chest and arms. His fingers brushed over her breasts and nipples, skimming down her belly, scorching a trail over her skin everywhere they touched her and making her tingle from head to toe.

She'd never met a man she moved in such perfect sync with. There was no awkwardness to their movements, no clumsiness as they tried to match each other's actions. They simply seemed to fall into an easy rhythm, recognizing exactly where they needed to be, where they each should move to be there to respond in time or shift out of the way.

His fingers hooked into her panties and shoved them down. She barely managed to shimmy out of them before his hands were at her hips, his fingers digging into the soft flesh there, scorching her skin. He picked her up as if she weighed nothing and lifted her up onto the edge of the desk.

She braced her hands there as he pulled away, reaching for his pants on the floor. She didn't take her eyes off of him, drinking in the sight of him, his firm buttocks flexing as he walked, his muscles shifting beneath taut skin. He was beautiful. There was no other word for it, for him. His body was lean and tight. A light layer of dark hair dusted his chest and the ridges of his belly, trailing lower from his belly button to where the proof of his arousal rose from his body, hard and thick and pulsing.

Digging into his wallet, he came up with a condom. Within seconds he had the package ripped open and covered himself. He turned back to her, taking one step before suddenly stopping, his eyes feasting on her. And as she watched the pure male appreciation play across his face, she'd never felt more desirable, or more desired.

Then he was back in front of her, his erection jutting forward, leading the way to her. His hands returned to her hips, the tip of his arousal unerringly finding her folds, primed to receive him, needing him inside her.

In the split second before it happened, his eyes moved to hers, meeting her gaze. Those dark eyes she'd thought were unreadable so many times burned with desire, the emotion undeniable and aimed squarely at her.

He thrust into her, hard, deep, in one push. Her eyes drifted shut, a moan rising in her throat, at the sensation of him filling her, at the pleasure, at the rightness of it. It was good. So very good. Her mouth fell open, the moan nearly slipping out. And then his mouth was on hers, claiming it again, swallowing the sound. His tongue dived back between her lips, stroking against hers, even as his hips pulled back and he thrust again, driving another groan from deep inside her.

She hooked her legs around his hips and dug her heels into his thighs, spurring him to move faster, deeper. He did, gradually picking up speed. She rocked against him, matching his rhythm with her lower body, meeting him every step of the way. As the pressure began building low in her body, starting where their bodies met, she wound her arms around him and held him to her tightly. It felt as if they were connected everywhere—their mouths, their limbs, their hips—and were truly one. She struggled to hold on as long as she could, even when it seemed as though the pressure was more than she could bear and there was no way she could hold on any longer, even as he pushed her higher and higher. She wanted more, wanted to put off that sweet release as long as possible, wanted this to last forever.

Until finally, incredibly, overwhelmingly, with one final hard thrust, she erupted. She clung to him, her fingers digging into his shoulders as wave after powerful wave ripped through her, obliterating every thought and sense in her mind, every bone and limb of her body in a rush of sheer pleasure. She distantly felt his body tensing beneath her hands, felt him go rigid in her arms, as he found his own release with her.

He sagged against her, his head dropping onto her shoulder. He remained there, leaning into her, still buried inside her. After a few long moments, he pressed the gentlest of kisses against her collarbone. The tenderness of it, the sweetness, sent another wave of feeling pooling through her, filling her with a fresh and entirely different kind of warmth. A sigh of contentment, of happiness, of so much more than she could begin to process, welled in her lungs.

The blistering, frenzied, desperate need that had overtaken them had faded, their passion satisfied. In its wake was a quiet intimacy that was even sweeter.

He continued to kiss his way along her collarbone, up her neck, finally reaching her mouth.

Their lips met, softly this time, but no less eager, the kiss long and lingering and utterly perfect.

It ended too soon. He finally broke the kiss, leaning back. She braced herself for him to pull away, not ready for it to happen.

It didn't. He stopped, still leaning over her, peering straight into her eyes, the look in them sparking the fire in her all over again. And she knew she'd been wrong. Her passion for him hadn't been satisfied. Not really. Not completely.

I will never get enough of this man, she realized with a sense of wonder.

He remained there, looking into her eyes, his hard features softened with feeling. And she realized something else.

He wasn't ready to pull away, either.

"This is crazy," he said again, his voice hoarse with feeling.

"I know," she whispered, sheer joy soaring through her. He wasn't talking about what they'd just done or the depth of the attraction that had led to it. He meant this, this indefinable connection between them that went beyond simple desire, that she now knew he felt, too. The sense that they were bound together. The urge to hold on and not let go.

A slow grin curved the corner of his lips. Of astonishment. Of happiness. Of acceptance.

And he lowered his mouth to hers once more.

Chapter Thirteen

"We should get dressed."

Lying next to him on the rug beside his desk, Jillian sighed against his chest. "I know."

She made no move to do so. Neither did Adam. It felt too good lying there, touching her, feeling her body against his, basking in the feeling of what they'd just shared. He'd known they should get dressed when he'd pushed away from her on the desk, had almost said it then. Instead he'd found himself lowering her to the floor, stretching out beside her, kissing her again, unable to let her go. Just as he couldn't now.

She ran her hand idly over his chest, the sensation of her soft fingers distracting him anew.

They lay in a comfortable silence for a few moments before Jillian finally spoke. "Meredith told me you blame yourself for what happened with her husband," she said softly.

Familiar anger swelled in his gut at the thought of that bastard, killing some of the pleasure of her nearness. "For good reason. I should have realized what was happening. We always spoke at least every week. Suddenly she stopped calling or messaging. I was so caught up in work I didn't even notice. I went weeks, even a couple months, without talking to my sister without even realizing it. That's on me." He'd been traveling so much, working a minimum of sixty hours a week, and for what? He'd turned into his father—something he'd never wanted to do—and only realized it when it was too late.

"Did you have any reason to believe her husband was capable of that before then?"

"I never liked him. He was too cocky, too full of himself. I thought he was all wrong for her. I just didn't recognize the meanness beneath the arrogance. That part he hid well, at least from the outside." Meredith was the one who'd had to deal with it firsthand. Alone. "He seemed to make her happy, so I tried to put my misgivings aside and didn't say anything." But he should have stayed on his guard, should have still paid attention.

"But you did help her. You managed to get her out of there."

"Only after he broke her jaw." The memory sent a hard lump to his throat, the horror of it still overwhelming his anger. "I called and tried to speak with her. The bastard tried putting me off, made excuses, and I immediately knew something was wrong. I took the first flight to Chicago—that's where they lived—and that's when I found out she was in the hospital. One of the neighbors had to tell me, a lady who drove her to the hospital when she couldn't. She——" He swallowed hard. "It wasn't just her jaw. He gave her a black eye and she had bruises all over. He damn near broke her shoulder——" The words caught, the images still vivid in his memory more than a year later. Just as it did every time he remembered, the guilt struck, raw and agonizing, square in his gut.

Jillian reached out and took his hand, squeezing tightly. From the way her body had tensed, he could tell she was picturing it. "Why wasn't he in jail?"

"She refused to say anything to the police or social workers when they tried to talk to her. Everyone knew who had done it—her neighbor told me it wasn't the first time, though it was the worst—but without Meredith's cooperation they couldn't do anything about it."

"Why didn't she want to tell them what happened?"

Because that was Meredith. Meredith, his shy, quiet little sister, who always tried to make people happy, who never made a fuss, so eager to please those she could never satisfy. Not their father, who'd never been around enough to notice his children's existence. Not their self-absorbed mother, who'd never considered anything her children did good enough.

Not a husband who took his own failings in life out on her, who didn't deserve her love.

"It would have been hard on her," Adam said, keeping his answer vague. "Having to relive it all again."

"So where is he now?" Jillian asked.

"Still in Chicago. She divorced him, though he actually tried to fight it."

"Whatever it took, at least she's away from him now."

"Yeah." But it didn't erase what had happened. Didn't take away the fact that Adam hadn't been there when she needed him most.

Jillian must have heard the self-recrimination in that single syllable. After a moment she said quietly, "I'm the last one who should be telling you not to blame yourself. I know what it's like to feel like you've failed someone you should have been there for."

Adam had no trouble understanding exactly what she meant. "Your friend must have meant a lot to you."

"She did. She *does*," Jillian corrected furiously. "We may not have been related by blood, but she was my sister in every way that matters. I told you I don't have any family? Well, she was the closest thing I had. Ever since grade school, when we were six years old on the playground."

"What about your parents?" he asked gently.

"It was just my mother and me. My father didn't stick around, and my mother wasn't exactly happy to be stuck with me. Half the time she forgot I existed. When I left home, we were basically done with each other. I don't even know where she is now. I haven't spoken to her in years."

"I'm sorry," he said, meaning it.

"It's all right. I had Courtney. Growing up I spent more time at her house than mine. Her parents were great. Probably not a surprise that she always dreamed of getting married, and I didn't." She grew quiet. "They both passed away within a few years of each other not long ago. But we still had each other. We might have lived in different cities and not have gotten to see each other as much, but she was still my best friend. My sister."

He didn't want her words or the pain in her voice to get to him. He wanted to tell her it wasn't the same. But it would be a lie. She'd loved Courtney Miller like a sister, and someone had hurt her sister. Not just hurt her, but killed her. Made it so that she would never have a chance to see her again. Adam had damn near killed Brad as it was. If that bastard had managed to kill Meredith, Adam knew there was nothing he wouldn't have done to get justice for her.

Just as Jillian was trying to do.

"I should have been here," she said hoarsely. "She gave me the only family I ever had, and I couldn't even be here for her when she needed me. But I can be here for her now. I can find out who did this to her. If you'll let me. Are you going to make me go?"

There it was, the question he'd been dreading. Because he knew the answer, and he didn't like it one bit. "I should," he said finally. For her own sake. For her safety.

He felt her smile, and knew she'd read the true answer in his response. "But you won't."

He couldn't, even if he thought she'd go easily. "No. I want to get to the bottom of this as much as you do." And knowing how much this meant to her, why she cared so much, he couldn't bring himself to make her leave.

Even as a small part of him whispered that he had his own selfish reasons for wanting her to stay.

"So what do you want to do?" she asked.

Another good question. "We can call the police. Tell them what happened to you and ask them to reopen the investigation into Courtney's death based on what we now know."

"I don't have any proof. Do you really think

they'll believe me, or will they just try to dismiss everything that's happened as a dream or a mere accident? I know they were told that Courtney was afraid of heights, but somehow they came to the conclusion she was not only on a high balcony at night, but came close enough to fall over." She made a sound of contempt in the back of her throat. "Come on. I wouldn't trust these cops to help a little old lady cross the street."

Truth be told, the more he thought about it, the less he could argue with her. The local police were just a small-town force, who likely didn't have much experience investigating major crimes. Then again, it wasn't as though the two of them did, either.

"Besides," she continued before he could point that out, "even if the police do question the staff, do you really think any of them is going to admit anything? They'll just know that we're onto them, and it'll be harder for us to figure out who it is. I know we can do this. After a few days here I bet I know more about these people than the police do, and you've been working with them for almost a year. We should be able to figure this out."

It had to be one of the staff. He recognized that, even if he still couldn't quite wrap his head around it. "Who was upstairs when you were pushed?"

"Ray and Zack were working in the ballroom.

I think Ed was supposed to be around some-where, too. Grace is the one who took me up there, though I don't know if she was still on the second floor. That's all I know of for sure, but if there are passageways in the west wing as well—and I have to believe there are—then anyone could have gotten up to that hallway and come up behind me."

"And anyone could have been the one who came into your room as well." He let out a sigh of frustration. "I just can't imagine why any one of them would want to stop the weddings."

"How much do you really know about the staff?"

"Mostly that they'd all been here for years. I did standard background checks on them when we decided to open the manor for weddings and keep them on, normal business procedure. None of them have criminal records, and since everyone but Zack had been here for decades there wasn't really any employment history to check out. Zack's background check was clean. I can't say I know any of them all that well per-sonally, but there didn't seem to be any reason they shouldn't be allowed to work here. If any-thing, they seemed to fit the atmosphere of the place, and Meredith didn't feel right about let-ting them go."

"I get the impression Grace isn't all that

pleased to no longer be in charge around here. It might be enough to make her want to stop the weddings."

"But without the weddings, we'll probably sell and she'd have to leave anyway."

"Maybe it's worth it to her. I don't know. There's more, though. I think Grace was in love with Jacob Sutton."

Adam was suddenly reminded of how he'd been struck by her use of Jacob's first name yesterday, the way she'd said it. "What makes you say that?"

"I think it's why she stayed here all these years. That comment she made at dinner about Kathleen being 'irreplaceable.' I think she wanted to be with Jacob, and he was still in love with his wife. Maybe Grace doesn't want to see any other woman get married here when she was denied the chance."

Adam considered the idea. "Pretty twisted motive."

"I think it's clear we're dealing with a very twisted mind here."

He couldn't exactly argue with that. "True. So you think it's her?"

"I think it *could* be. But all of them seem to have issues that, in theory, could make them want to stop the weddings. I mean, Ed and Rosie *are* married, but don't seem happy about it. Talking to her the other day, I got the impression she's not too happy to be married to him. Probably not a surprise considering how she treats him. And I know he's usually all smiles, but I've seen the way he looks at her sometimes. It's…cold, calculating. Not the way I can imagine anyone looking at someone they love. Then there's Ray. Did you know his wife abandoned him and Zack?"

"No," he admitted.

"Either one of them—or both—could have substantial enough issues with women that they'd go after women who are getting married."

"So that leaves us with what we already knew. It could be any one of them." He couldn't keep the frustration out of his voice. "Maybe I should call the company I had run the background checks, have them run more in-depth checks on them in case there's anything else we should know that we don't already." Perhaps he should have dug deeper to begin with, but it hadn't seemed necessary. He'd basically been hiring people to work at a hotel, not the Pentagon. He hadn't needed to know more about them. Or so he'd thought.

"Good idea."

"In the meantime, every moment you're here you'll be a target."

She fell quiet for a moment. "We could still use that to our advantage."

Adam immediately recoiled at the idea. "I am not going to let you use yourself as bait," he said firmly.

"If we can draw out the killer, we can catch him or her."

"Or you can get yourself killed. This person already managed to get to you twice."

"I didn't have anyone watching my back. And now I do."

She said it as a statement of plain fact, not a question, as though she had no doubt that he would be there for her. She was right, of course, and her faith in him nearly made his chest swell with a sense of masculine pride, regardless of why she was saying it.

"Yeah," he said roughly. "You do. And I'm watching your back when I say you're not using yourself as bait. We'll figure something out."

Jillian nodded once. "All right. What about Meredith? Do you want to tell her the truth about me?"

Adam considered the question. It was another one he didn't like the answer to. "I don't like the idea of leaving her clueless to what's really going on here, but Meredith isn't the best liar. Never has been. I think it's one reason she became so distant when things went bad with that bastard

Brad. She had to know I would realize what was going on. And she hasn't been that strong emotionally in the wake of everything that happened. If we do tell her, I'm not sure she would be able to keep from letting the others know something is up."

"So we won't tell her yet," Jillian agreed. "Hopefully we'll be able to tell her soon enough, if we can resolve this quickly."

Which they would, he thought. Whoever was responsible for all of this had to be stopped before anything else happened, anyone else was hurt.

Now, if they could only figure out how to do that.

In the meantime... "We really should get dressed before anyone comes looking for us."

Adam felt her sigh, and nearly did the same. "You're right."

With mutual reluctance, they pushed apart and climbed to their feet. They dressed quickly, collecting the clothes they'd scattered across the floor and shrugging into them. Adam couldn't resist sneaking a few glimpses of her tantalizing body as it was regrettably recovered—and found her looking back at him, watching him in exactly the same way.

Jillian shot him a grin, completely unembarrassed to be caught staring or to have him look. He could only grin back.

God, she was amazing. So vital, so full of life. Just the idea of anything happening to this woman—

Not going to happen, he vowed.

Finally, all too soon, they were dressed. Unable to resist, he reached for her, moving in for another kiss.

A sharp knock suddenly sounded on the door. They barely had time to move away from each other, let alone acknowledge the knock, before the door swung open. "Hey, boss—"

It was Zack. He came to an abrupt stop just inside the doorway as though sensing he'd interrupted something. He glanced between the two of them, eyes narrowing.

Adam could imagine what he saw. They hadn't taken the time to completely straighten their clothes and hair, so they had to look disheveled, as if they'd been—well, as if they'd been doing exactly what they had.

"What is it, Zack?" Adam asked, keeping his tone completely unconcerned.

Zack lowered his eyes, his discomfort clear. "We're finished in the ballroom, but Ed is worried part of the basement might flood with all this rain. Looks like there's already some leakage. He wanted to know if you wanted to come take a look so you'd know what was going on."

"Thanks, Zack," Adam said. "I'll be right out."

Zack nodded tightly. Ducking his head, he backed out of the room, closing the door behind him.

As soon as it was shut, Jillian raked a hand through her hair, giving it a makeshift combing. "I don't suppose there's any chance he's *not* going to tell everyone what he just saw—or thinks he saw."

"I doubt it. I'd give it about thirty minutes, tops, before everyone knows."

"The only question is, how will the killer react?"

"If they think this means your wedding is off, they might be happy," he suggested.

Jillian's frown deepened. "But then they might not come after me again and we'll never know who it is."

"There has to be another way to get to the bottom of this without making you a target."

"I'm all ears."

Grimacing, he shot a glance at the window, listening to the wind and rain pounding against the glass. "We'll figure it out. In the meantime, let me put in a call to my investigator and get that ball rolling. And then let's just try to get through this storm without anyone getting hurt."

Chapter Fourteen

Zack was waiting by the stairs in the front entry-way when they came out of the office. Leaning against the banister with his arms folded over his chest, he looked up at their approach and slowly straightened.

As they came closer, Adam studied the younger man, considering what he knew about him. It wasn't much. Zack was only twenty-four. He'd lived in Hawthorne and at Sutton Hall for most of his life, except for a year he'd spent in Boston not long ago. He didn't have a criminal record or any signs of trouble in his past. Adam had hired him mostly because Ray had asked him to and because he obviously knew the estate better than anyone else Adam could have found.

Now, though, he had to wonder if he'd made a mistake, especially when Zack's gaze slid to Jillian, his mouth twisting with contempt before he glanced away.

His anger spiking, Adam speared the man

with a glare. Under different circumstances, he might have dealt with the man's attitude more diplomatically, but he wasn't in the mood to play nice. "Everything all right, Zack?"

Zack grimaced, not looking directly at him. "Fine."

"If you have something you want to say, maybe you should just say it."

Zack clenched his jaw. "It's none of my business."

"You're right," Adam said. "But I think we'd like to hear what you have to say anyway."

Zack finally turned that contemptuous glare on Adam. "All right." He looked straight at Jillian, his lip curling in a sneer. "Guess commitments don't mean that much to you after all, huh?"

Jillian simply looked back at him steadily. "Are you upset because you think something happened between Adam and me, or because I didn't take you up on your offer?"

"My 'offer' wasn't serious," Zack scoffed. "I just wanted to see how serious *you* were about getting married. Turns out, you're not. You're even worse than the last one. At least she never did anything."

Adam felt Jillian tense beside him. "You mean the first bride to come here?" she asked.

"Yeah. I saw the way she looked at me. Couldn't

take her eyes off me, all while she was supposed to be planning her wedding." He shook his head. "Commitments don't mean that much to anybody, do they?"

"You mean like they didn't to your mother?"

Zack's eyes narrowed to slits. "Don't call her that. She doesn't deserve the title."

"There could have been other reasons why she left," Jillian said gently. "You don't know—"

"Yeah, I do," Zack snapped. "I managed to track her down last year. She said sorry, but she wasn't cut out to be a mother and getting married was the worst mistake she ever made. She never should have done it and she never did again after she left." He snorted. "Maybe she should have figured that out before she bothered doing it the first time. It would have been a hell of a lot better on my dad and me if she had. The same way it would be for the guy you're supposed to be marrying if you end it now."

"If that's how you feel, I'm surprised you wanted to work around weddings and brides," Adam said coolly. "Maybe you'd be happier working somewhere else."

Zack shrugged a shoulder. "You're right about that. Go ahead and fire me. Just do me a favor and fire my dad, too. The only reason I came back here was to convince him to stop hiding on this damned mountain and get out of here.

He needs to start living, not let his life be ruined by somebody who isn't worth it." With one last scornful glance at Jillian, he turned and stormed off down the hall.

"What do you think?" Adam asked softly when they were alone again. "Is he our killer?"

"He's certainly angry. I just don't know if he'd be that upfront with his contempt for me or Courtney, or his reasons why, if he is the killer."

"He might be if he was completely out of control, the way the killer has to be."

"Did he seem that unhinged to you?"

"No," Adam admitted, not particularly happy about it. It would be easier if he could believe Zack obviously was their killer. It would mean this nightmare was finally over, that Jillian was out of danger. But even when Zack was clearly angry, Adam hadn't sensed any real danger or threat of violence from him.

"I'd been wondering what really happened to Ray's wife," Jillian said quietly. "Guess now I know."

"If Zack was telling the truth."

"True," Jillian agreed. "Though his story does make sense. It explains why he came back when he doesn't really like the job and the librarian in town told me he always wanted to leave the area."

"Well, he won't have to worry about the job for long," Adam said grimly.

Jillian glanced up at him. "So you're going to fire him?"

"I don't think I have much of a choice."

"And Ray?"

He sighed. "I don't know. It might be for the best, though I don't know if it's fair to him."

Before Jillian could respond, the sound of approaching footsteps reached them. A few seconds later, Meredith stepped into the foyer.

As soon as she spotted them she came to an abrupt stop. "Oh," she exhaled in surprise. "I was just coming to check on you, Jillian."

Adam didn't miss the way her eyes slid between him and Jillian, a contemplative—and apprehensive—gleam in them. He doubted Zack had a chance to tell her that he'd found the two of them together. Could she sense something had changed between them, or did she just still have the same suspicions she'd had earlier?

"I'm sure the two of you have a lot of work to do," Adam said. "If you'll excuse me, I need to check on a situation in the basement."

Meredith's eyebrows raised. "Everything all right?"

Fighting a twinge of guilt at keeping the truth from her, he worked up a smile. "Nothing to worry about from the sounds of it."

He met Jillian's eyes. She nodded shortly before turning toward Meredith. "Should we finally check out the ballroom?" she asked with a smile.

Adam watched them go for a moment, fighting the unease rising in his gut. He wouldn't be gone long, and they should be safe together. But as they disappeared from view, it took everything he had not to follow. The thought of anything happening to either one of them was unimaginable. He'd let Meredith be hurt far too much for one lifetime. And Jillian... He'd just found her.

He couldn't let anything happen to either one of them.

More importantly, he wasn't going to.

DINNER WAS EVEN more uncomfortable than usual, tension lying thick and heavy over the dining room. At the head of the table, Adam sat as grim and remote as a statue, seemingly deep in thought. Even Meredith made no attempt at conversation, leaving the meal to pass in uneasy silence.

Jillian figured the storm was the main reason for it. The dining room curtains were drawn tight, but they couldn't completely block out the sound of the raging wind and the lash of the rain on the glass. The noises were loud in the relative quiet of the room, making it impossible to forget that nature was raging all around them.

Still, she had to wonder if that was the only

reason, or if Zack had told anyone how he'd found her and Adam together.

Rosie avoided looking at anyone as she served the meal, a heavy frown on her rounded face. But she'd been the same way that morning when Jillian had seen her at breakfast, her mood edgy and distracted, so Jillian didn't know if she could read anything new into the woman's behavior.

As for Grace...

Even as she thought it, Jillian suddenly sensed someone was watching her.

She looked up and met Grace's eyes.

It wasn't the first time Jillian had caught the woman looking at her. Grace's cool gaze was steady and appraising, her face as stoic as ever. After a moment, she slowly lowered her attention back to her plate.

But not before Jillian caught the subtle change in her expression, the knowing gleam in her eye.

A sudden chill rolled through her from both the knowledge and the look she'd seen in the woman's stare.

She knows.

It was all Jillian could do not to reflexively reach out and straighten her clothes further, fully aware it would only make things look worse. There wasn't a doubt in her mind Grace knew about her and Adam. And if Zack had told Grace, it was likely he'd told Rosie, too, and it was only a matter of time before Ray and Ed found out, too, if they hadn't already.

Which left the question of what the killer would think—or do.

"Mr. Sutton."

The voice was like a clap of thunder in the stillness, nearly making Jillian flinch. Everyone in the room turned toward the sound.

Ed stood in the doorway, water dripping from his clothes, his normally smiling face even more serious than the last time Jillian had seen him.

"Ed?" Adam said, already pushing away from the table. "What happened?"

"I was checking the upper floors in the west wing. We've got a tree down. It busted straight through a window in one of the back bedrooms on the second floor. I tried dislodging it, but it's pretty well stuck. The rain's coming straight in, and it's hard to tell, but I think the tree might have done some damage to the wall."

His face grim with purpose, Adam moved to join the man. "Where are Ray and Zack?"

"I don't know. I'm looking for them, too."

Grace rose from her seat. "I'll help find them."

"Thanks, Grace," Adam said. "Please send them up when you do. I'm going to head up with Ed to see how bad it is."

With a nod, Grace moved toward the kitchen.

"Is there anything I can do?" Meredith asked.

"No," Adam said. "You and Jillian stay here. We can take care of it."

"I can help, too," Jillian suggested.

"No," he said, a little sharper than necessary. "Just stay here with Meredith."

Jillian didn't take offense at his tone, reading the warning in his stare too clearly. She understood. In the middle of a chaotic situation, with everyone dealing with the mess and both of them distracted, it might be too easy for somebody to try to do something to her. She couldn't exactly be on her guard if she was focused on trying to help, and she wouldn't be much help if she was trying to watch her back at the same time. She was better off staying with Meredith, where she'd ostensibly be safer.

"All right," she murmured.

She didn't miss the flash of relief that briefly passed over his face. She waited, expecting him to turn and leave. He paused, and she sensed his sudden reluctance to go, his eyes sending her an unmistakable message.

Be careful, they seemed to say.

Jillian gave a tiny, barely perceptible nod. *I will.*

A heartbeat later, he turned back to the other man. "Okay, Ed. Show me where it is."

The two men quickly made their way out of

the room. Jillian watched Adam go, her heart feeling uncommonly heavy in her chest. It was a strange feeling having someone looking out for her. She was so used to being on her own, she couldn't remember the last time someone had looked at her with any concern that was more than mere politeness.

There was nothing polite about the worry in Adam's eyes. He genuinely cared about her well-being. Jillian understood the feeling. Even though she knew he wasn't really facing a dangerous situation, she couldn't deny the flicker of unease that struck low in her belly as he disappeared from view.

"I'm sure they can handle it, especially with Ray and Zack to help," Meredith said, perhaps misreading the worry on Jillian's face. "Why don't we go into the living room? We can talk about ideas on how to use the outdoor space."

Jillian forced a smile. "Great."

As they prepared to leave the room, she did her best to put Adam out of her mind. He had a job to do, but so did she. Solving Courtney's murder.

That was what she needed to focus on.

ONE GLIMPSE IN the room Ed had led him to was all it took for Adam to see the situation was even worse than he'd imagined. The tree was massive, practically filling the entire space of what had once been a sizable window, a mess of branches and leaves jutting several feet into the room. Adam didn't doubt that an object that huge must have done some damage to the wall beneath the window when it had crashed into it, though it was hard to tell how bad it was with the tree in the way. Rain seemed to pour in through every spot that wasn't taken up by the tree, water drenching the floor and spraying across the room. Beyond it, the sky was so dark it might as well have been the dead of night.

"Damn," Adam muttered under his breath.

The word was nearly lost in the wind that rushed into the room and lashed at them. Ed clearly heard it just the same, grunting in response. "Yep."

"What do you recommend?" Adam asked, fully prepared to rely on the man's expertise.

Ed eyed the tree solemnly, his cheek working as he considered the problem. "It's too big and too heavy to push out. I already tried that. We'll probably have to take a look from outside, cut it out there so we can push it out. Maybe break off as many of the branches in here as we can so it'll be easier to move, too."

"Then it's just a matter of the window and the wall."

Ed waved off the comment. "I can handle that. Getting this thing out of here is my main concern."

The sound of feet pounding down the hall reached them. Adam glanced back just as Ray and Zack appeared in the doorway.

The two men came to an abrupt stop just inside the room, staring in disbelief at the sight that met their eyes. Zack swore lightly.

"As you can see, we have quite a job to deal with," Adam told them. "I hate to ask it of you, but I think I'm going to need you outside on this." He quickly explained the plan Ed had outlined. "If we work together both inside and out, we should be able to get the tree out of here."

"Makes sense," Ray said simply, with no trace of rancor. "And taking care of the trees is my job."

"Good," Adam said. "I'll come with you. With the three of us working, we should be able to get the tree cut and possibly pulled out. Ed will stay here to break off the branches and prepare to deal with the window as soon as the tree's out." He paused, a thought occurring to him. "We'll need to keep in contact on both ends. Do you all have phones on you?"

"I do," Zack said.

Ed and Ray shook their heads.

"Mine's in my office," Adam told Ed. "I'll

bring it back up here for you and we'll call you from Zack's phone so we can communicate what's happening." He just had to hope they'd be able to get a workable cell signal in this weather. If not, they'd have to figure out another system, with someone probably running back and forth, which would take far more time.

"Sounds good," Ed acknowledged.

"Great. Let's do it."

Leaving Ed behind, Adam broke for the door with the other two. He didn't exactly relish the idea of heading out into the storm, but he didn't have a choice. It was a big job, one that would require as many hands as possible. Sutton Hall was his responsibility. He couldn't sit by and leave its welfare in the hands of others when his help was needed. Even if it meant venturing out into the wind and rain.

Even if it meant being unable to watch out for Jillian while he was out there.

She's fine, he told himself. *She's with Meredith. They're both fine.*

But telling himself that didn't do anything to ease the dread he could feel pooling in his belly at the thought.

"What about something like this?"

Seated on a sofa across from Meredith, Jillian looked up to find the other woman holding up a magazine for her to see. "Oh, that's nice," she said. "Let's keep that one in mind."

Smiling, Meredith marked the page and turned it to the next.

Jillian returned her attention to the magazine in her own lap, not absorbing it any more than whatever Meredith had just shown her. She did her best to look as if she was perusing it for wedding ideas the way she was supposed to, trying not to let her restlessness show.

Outside, the wind seemed to have picked up, the frenzied howling matching the churning in her gut. She'd meant what she'd told Adam. She believed they could figure this out. She just needed to figure out how.

Perhaps his investigator would find something. In the meantime, she had to try to get the staff to open up to her more, as unlikely as that seemed. Unfortunately, with everyone busy dealing with the storm, she'd probably have to wait until it was over to find out for sure. Which left her biding her time, sitting here when all she wanted was to be doing something, anything at all.

"Excuse me."

Jillian raised her head at the sound of the voice. Rosie stood in the entryway. In her hands she balanced a tray bearing a teapot, a small pitcher and two cups.

"I heard about the commotion," she said, her

expression still tense and grim. "I thought you could use some tea."

"That actually sounds wonderful," Meredith said. "Thank you, Rosie."

With a curt nod, the woman crossed the room and placed the tray on the table between them. Straightening, she glanced warily at the window on the far wall. "Tea's good for a day like this. Calms the nerves."

"Do you have a lot of days like this around here?" Jillian asked.

"Sometimes," Rosie said distantly. "In the spring. This one's worse than most, though." With a shudder, she turned away from the window. "I need to get dinner cleaned up." Her face still creased with worry, she strode from the room.

Jillian studied the scene outside the window. Rosie was right. It was bad out there, virtually pitch-black. Jillian was pretty sure it had gotten worse, the wind howling louder, the rain pelting the glass like bullets. It barely seemed like the window should be able to withstand the onslaught, as though it would shatter at any moment.

Like the window upstairs had when the tree came through it. She wondered how Adam was doing, how bad the situation was up there.

"Would you like a cup?"

Jillian looked back at Meredith. Having poured a cup for herself, she had the pot poised over the other.

Jillian wasn't much of a tea drinker, but at the moment something to calm her nerves didn't sound so bad. "I'd love one."

Meredith proceeded to pour. "Milk?"

"No, thank you."

Setting the pot down, Meredith offered the cup and saucer to Jillian.

Taking them, Jillian raised the cup to her lips for a small, experimental taste. Not bad.

As she let the warmth of the tea sink into her system, she glanced back at the window. She really could see nothing outside. It was as if the rest of the world had ceased to exist, making them seem even more isolated out here than ever.

Isolated with a killer.

Suppressing a shudder, Jillian turned away from the glass. She would certainly be glad when the storm was over, for more than one reason.

As soon as Adam reached the first floor with Ray and Zack, he moved toward his office. "I'll meet you both out there as soon as I can," he told them.

Nodding, father and son headed toward the back to retrieve their coats.

Adam quickly made his way to his office. His

cell phone was on the desk where he'd left it. Picking it up, he checked the battery level. He couldn't remember the last time he'd charged it. He had to hope it had enough power left—

The landline on the desktop suddenly rang.

He was prepared to ignore it when he remembered the call he'd placed to his investigator earlier. He'd had to leave a message. This might be them calling back. He really would like to get them started on the background checks as soon as possible.

He reached for the phone. "Sutton Hall."

"This is Vince at Best In Class Rent-a-Car. I'm trying to reach Jillian Jones."

Adam frowned. Why was the man calling the house number? "Have you tried her cell phone?"

"Yes, sir, but I didn't get an answer and she left this number as a secondary contact so I thought I'd try it."

Of course. "I'm sorry, I'm not sure where she is right now. Can I take a message?"

"I just wanted to let her know we had the car checked out. It looks like somebody played a prank on her."

Adam froze. "What do you mean?"

"It appears somebody poured sugar in the gas tank, which clogged up the filter and caused the engine to stop running. Didn't do any damage to the engine, but was enough to get her stranded.

Stupid kid stuff. Doesn't even work half the time, but in this case, it did."

After everything that had happened to her, Adam didn't believe for a moment it had simply been a prank. Someone had deliberately sabotaged her car. But why?

"Thanks for calling," he said into the phone. "I'll definitely let her know."

Lowering the phone, he quickly thought back to the day her car had died. He wasn't the only one who'd been in town when someone would have tampered with the car, he remembered.

Ed was in town then, too.

Ed, who hadn't come back with the sugar Rosie had asked for.

It had to be him. But why would Ed want to sabotage Jillian's car? To try to hurt her? Was he the one behind everything that had happened to her since she arrived here?

Standing there thinking about it wasn't going to get him any answers. There was one surefire way that would.

Adam bolted for the door.

Leaving his office, he quickly headed to the living room, needing to check on Jillian, needing to know she was safe.

He peeked into the room, instantly spotting her. She and Meredith sat across from each other on separate sofas. Their heads were bowed over the magazines, papers and various items they had spread out in front of them.

A sigh of relief worked its way from his lungs. No point in disturbing them.

Jillian was safe with Meredith.

He needed to talk to Ed—now.

ADAM.

Jillian felt the prickle of recognition at the nape of her neck. Her heart lifting, she automatically glanced behind her toward the door to the room.

No one was there.

Jillian frowned as she took in the empty doorway. She could have sworn he was there, right behind her.

She nearly shook her head. The place must be getting to her. She was imagining things.

She felt Meredith glance over at her, then twist her neck to look toward the door. "What is it?" she asked.

"Nothing," Jillian said quickly. "Just thought I heard something."

With a shrug, she turned back to the magazine in front of her. She wasn't surprised she was imagining things. She was suddenly exhausted. Probably not a surprise given how little sleep she'd gotten the past few days, not to mention how much had happened today alone.

She gave her head a hard shake. She didn't have time to be tired. Not while Courtney's killer was still out there, still unidentified. She needed a plan.

Swallowing a yawn, Jillian willed herself to focus.

She had to figure this out.

ADAM FOUND ED where he'd left him in the room the tree had crashed into. He was breaking off some of the branches, leveraging his body weight against some of them to get them to weaken.

For a moment, Adam stood in the doorway and watched the man. He considered everything he knew—or thought he knew—about this man he'd worked with for a year. He was a good worker. Always pleasant, always had a smile. But a killer? Adam never would have guessed it.

"Ed, I need to talk to you."

The man stopped what he was doing and glanced back at him. "Got the phone?"

Adam looked down at the device in his hand, surprised to realize he'd forgotten all about it. "Yes, but that's not what I need to talk about."

"What is it?"

"The rental company Ms. Jones got her car

from called. They had the engine checked out to see why it stopped running. Do you know what they found?"

The utter stillness that gripped Ed's body, giving him the appearance of a trapped animal, told Adam he knew full well.

Ed dropped his head. "No," he mumbled. "Why would I?"

"Because you're the one who poured sugar in her gas tank, aren't you?"

The man didn't respond at first, swaying uneasily on his feet. "Don't know what you're talking about—"

He didn't even have the words out before Adam lunged forward in a burst of fury, getting right in the other man's face. "Don't you dare lie to me right now! Damn it, tell me the truth. Did you also push her down the stairs? Attack her in her room?"

Ed's eyes flared with alarm, with desperation. "No!"

"Why should I believe you?"

"I didn't want to hurt her! I was just trying to scare her a little. I just wanted her to go away."

"Why?" Adam demanded.

"She's not safe here."

"Right! From you!"

"No! That's not it. I was trying to protect her."

"Jillian?" It didn't make any sense.

"No, not her."

The man was talking in riddles. He was trying to protect somebody by sabotaging Jillian's car, but not Jillian herself. That only left one possibility. "Rosie?"

Ed finally looked Adam square in the eyes, his expression desperate and pleading. "You understand, don't you? A brother has to take care of his sister."

He wasn't making a damn bit of sense. "What the hell does your sister have to do with this?" Adam exploded.

The man's eyes skittered away, his shoulders slumping so that he looked thoroughly defeated.

Ed's words turned over and over in Adam's mind, a vague suspicion beginning to take hold. His first impulse was to reject it. It was ridiculous. It was crazy.

As crazy as a killer targeting brides at Sutton Hall.

With a creeping sense of dread, he knew he had to ask. He forced out the question.

"Ed, who is your sister?"

Focus.

Jillian had repeated the order so many times it was starting to lose all meaning. It certainly wasn't doing any good. If anything, she could barely keep her eyes open.

She opened her mouth to say something to Meredith, hoping the conversation could keep her awake, only to have a yawn emerge. Fighting it back, she realized it had been a while since Meredith had said anything, either. She glanced up at the other woman.

Meredith was slumped in her seat, her chin resting against her chest, her eyelids shut.

Frowning, Jillian stared at her. Meredith's chest rose and fell gently, her breathing deep and even. She was asleep.

That was strange. Meredith hadn't seemed that tired. Then again, Jillian really hadn't been, either. And now she was. So groggy.

No, something was wrong here, she realized, alarm starting to break through the fuzziness in her head. Something… Why couldn't she seem to think?

"I thought she'd never drift off," a voice said.

Jillian turned her head toward the speaker, a process that seemed to take an eternity. Why was she moving so slowly?

Rosie stood in the doorway again. She stared at Jillian blankly, her face wiped clean of all expression. But her eyes seemed cold. Furious, even.

At least that was what it looked like to Jillian, though she was having trouble focusing, the woman's face wavering slightly before her eyes.

"You wanted her to drift off?" she asked. Heck, even her voice seemed funny, her tongue feeling thick and fuzzy in her mouth.

"Of course. I needed her out of the way for this."

Only then did Jillian catch the open malice in the woman's steely tones, the sound sending a shiver of warning through her.

"And now I just have to take care of you."

Chapter Fifteen

"Rosie."

It was the answer Adam had somehow expected, but that still didn't mean it made a damn bit of sense.

He stared at the bowed head of the defeated man before him in disbelief. "What are you telling me?" he demanded. "Rosie's not your wife?"

"No," Ed confirmed sadly. "She just got to telling people that and I went along with it. Was easier than fighting with her and it made her happy. God knows, there were few enough things that could do that."

"Why would your sister tell people you were married?"

Ed sighed heavily. "Rosie always wanted to get married, ever since she was a little girl. Was always pretending to be walking down the aisle, talking about putting on that white dress, used to make me act like I was her groom and march around with her." He grimaced. "When she was nineteen she got engaged to this fellow in the town where we grew up. She was finally going to get that wedding she'd been talking about all those years. Except in the end he ran off with somebody else. Stood her up at the altar. I'll never forget what she looked like standing there when they told her he'd gone off with another woman. Like somebody'd ripped her heart out. I mean, that's basically what the guy did.

"She never got over it. She…had some troubles after that, tried to kill herself, started lashing out at people. She wasn't fit to be around people for a while. They took her away and put her in a home for a time. But after our folks died, I couldn't afford to keep her there, so I brought her home to keep an eye on her myself. But Porter, the man she was supposed to marry, had come back with the woman he ran off with and they were living there. When Rosie came back things got ugly, and I had to get us out of town."

Adam felt a flicker of disquiet thinking about just how "ugly" things must have gotten that they would have had to leave town.

"We started traveling around, looking for work where I could keep an eye on her and she could stay out of trouble. When we came here, it seemed perfect. Quiet. Out of the way. And when she saw that picture in the front hall of Mr. Sutton and his wife, she wanted to live here most of all. She told Mr. Sutton that we were married before I could say different, said she was humiliated having people know she was an old maid who needed her brother to take care of her. I didn't know how to tell him the truth without having to explain why Rosie would say something like that. We needed the work and I didn't want him to figure he wouldn't want us around. So I went along with it and let everybody think we were married. It was easy enough. We have the same last name and all. And it made her happy."

"What about you? Didn't you ever want to get married yourself, have a family of your own?"

"I never had time to think much about it. I had to take care of her. And frankly, after hearing her talk about weddings and marriage all this time, it kind of put me off the whole thing."

Adam supposed he couldn't blame him for that, but there were a hell of a lot of other things he could. "You had to know it was a bad idea to have her here once we started having weddings."

"I was hoping I could keep an eye on her well enough to keep her out of trouble. I was hoping it would be all right."

"You should have told me the truth."

"She's my sister. I was just trying to do right by her."

"What about the people she hurt? You obviously knew she was responsible for what happened to Courtney Miller."

"I didn't know for sure," the man protested weakly.

"But you had to suspect. And when Jillian 'fell' down the stairs? Did you know Rosie pushed her? Or was that you, trying to 'scare' her?"

"I wouldn't do that! I wasn't trying to hurt anybody."

"You were just willing to stand by and do nothing while Rosie did." As the man had implied earlier, Adam could certainly relate to the instinct to do right by his sister. But what the man had done—what he'd apparently let Rosie get away with—was in no way justifiable, sibling loyalty be damned.

From the way the man wouldn't look at him and didn't bother trying to defend himself, he knew it, too.

But Ed wasn't the real problem here. Knowing exactly how disturbed Rosie was, Adam was no longer sure Jillian could be safe as long as she wasn't alone. He didn't want Meredith anywhere near the woman, either.

A sense of foreboding suddenly filled him, every instinct going on alert.

"I need to find out where Rosie is. *Now.*"

JILLIAN STARED AT the woman in bewilderment. "What are you talking about?" she said weakly. Even her voice sounded faint. "Take care of me?"

Moving with an unmistakable sense of purpose, Rosie stalked toward her. "I can't let you go ahead and get married, can I? Not when you don't deserve it. Not when you're nothing but a tramp."

The words didn't make any sense. None of this made any sense. "I don't understand."

Before Jillian could protest, the woman bent down and hooked her arm around Jillian's back, hoisting her out of the chair and fully upright. Jillian couldn't seem to get her legs under her. It didn't seem to matter as Rosie practically carried her toward the door, Jillian's feet barely touching the ground.

"You're just like the last one," Rosie muttered, her voice thickening with anger. "No, you're worse. I saw the way she looked at Zack, with lust in her eyes. She was going to put on that beautiful white dress and marry someone when she was panting after somebody else. But at least she didn't go to bed with him. Unlike you. You slept with Adam, and you still sat there, planning your wedding, preparing to marry one man when you had the stink of another on you. *Whore*."

The woman's insults didn't even penetrate the

haze clouding Jillian's mind. The only thing that did was one stark fact. "You killed Courtney."

"I had no choice, now did I?" Rosie said, with what almost sounded like pride. "I couldn't let her desecrate the sanctity of marriage. I couldn't let her make a mockery of those sacred vows she clearly didn't respect. Neither of you deserve that ceremony. You don't deserve those vows. *I* did. I saved myself. I never looked at another man. And I never got that beautiful wedding. I never got to be a bride, or a wife."

"But you are married," Jillian protested, trying to make sense of the woman's rambling.

"Lies," Rosie hissed practically in her ear. "It's all lies. Lies so nobody would know my shame. I had to pretend Ed was my husband to keep anybody from knowing my disgrace. Knowing that I was living with my *brother,* that I didn't have a husband and never had. I had to live this pale imitation of a real woman's life, everybody thinking I had what I'd really been robbed of."

Ed wasn't her husband? This wasn't making any sense, along with so many other things. For instance— "What are you going to do to me?"

"I'm afraid you're going to take an unfortunate tumble down the basement stairs. They're so steep, I've always been afraid someone would fall and break their neck. Sadly, it's going to be you."

"You can't think you'll get away with this."

"Of course I will. Just like I did with the last one. Nobody figured out she didn't die in an accident, and no one will with you, either."

"*I* figured it out," Jillian declared. A surge of fury rushed through her, piercing the fuzziness in her head and giving her a brief burst of strength. "I didn't come here to get married. Courtney Miller was my best friend. I knew her death was no accident. I've told people back home about my investigation. If anything happens to me, they'll know it was no accident."

"But you didn't know it was me, otherwise you would have been more suspicious and you wouldn't have drunk the tea. That means no one else does, too."

"Someone will come along now. They'll see what you're doing."

"Everyone's busy dealing with that tree. Ray and Zack are outside. Ed and Adam are all the way upstairs on the other side of the house. Grace went to check the other rooms in the west wing to make sure there weren't any other problems that needed to be handled. And Meredith's taking a nap."

"They'll still know it wasn't an accident. They'll find the drug in my bloodstream. They'll know I didn't just fall."

"By the time anyone finds you, most of it should be out of your bloodstream. And I'll leave some of the pills in your luggage so they'll think the drugs were yours anyway. Too bad you took some before you decided to snoop."

"But they'll know Meredith was drugged, too."

"Obviously *you* did that, to give yourself time to snoop. After all, the pills are yours."

They'd made it to the dining room. Rosie tsked softly under her breath. "You've only given me one more reason why you have to die. Pretending to be a bride? You really have no shame, do you? No respect for what that means."

Clearly there was not going to be any reasoning with the woman. She was completely insane. Jillian's only chance was to fight back physically, not with mere words. She struggled to force her limbs into compliance. She got only the barest flicker of response. They felt numb, almost as if they were no longer attached to her body. Panic rose inside her the more she struggled to get any kind of reaction from them. She didn't believe Adam would believe this was an accident or there was any way Rosie would get away with this. But that wouldn't do Jillian any good if she was dead.

"That might actually make this work better," Rosie muttered under her breath. "It's going to look suspicious to have another bride die around here. But if you're not really a bride then it won't look so strange. Everyone already knows you've been poking your nose around here, going places you don't belong. It only makes sense that you'd try to go down to the basement. These stairs are steep. Anybody would trip and fall on them. Too bad for you that you decided to sneak down there when everyone was busy with the storm."

At this point Jillian suspected the woman was no longer trying to convince her. Rosie was simply talking to herself, her frenzied ramblings only deepening the impression that she'd gone that far over the edge.

They finally reached the kitchen, Rosie pushing through the revolving door. Jillian immediately spotted the open door Rosie began guiding her to.

The doorway to the basement.

It stood black and empty. Waiting for her.

Frantically, Jillian tried harder to get her limbs to move. She felt the faintest, tiniest trace of response in her arms and legs. She worked harder, trying to build her strength, trying not to give her efforts away. Maybe the woman would think she'd finally passed out, maybe she would lower her guard. Jillian needed her to, needed every advantage she could get. She might have only one chance to strike, only one shot to fight the woman off.

She finally felt her muscles begin to tighten,

her strength gathering, wanting to lash out. She couldn't do it too soon. She needed just the right moment. She would need every last bit of strength, even if she wondered if there was really any way she could fight the woman off, any way she could prevent her from throwing her down those stairs…

The door came ever closer. Jillian's terror climbed with each step that brought them nearer.

This was it. She had to do it. She'd have to use whatever strength she had. The door was only ten feet away.

Then five.

Three—

"Rosie, stop!"

Adam. Jillian recognized the voice immediately, joy and relief and excitement exploding inside her in a giddy rush. He was here. He'd found her.

Her body tensing in shock, Rosie whirled around, pulling Jillian with her, in front of her—

So she no longer faced the basement door.

Rosie's hold relaxed the slightest bit.

Now.

Adrenaline surging, Jillian jerked her leg up and stomped hard on Rosie's foot. At the same moment, she threw her elbows back, driving them hard into the woman's gut, propelling herself forward.

With a screech, Rosie's hold loosened entirely, releasing her.

Jillian tumbled forward, the floor rushing toward her. Her legs flying upward, she kicked out to ward the woman off further, making contact one more time.

She landed hard on her belly, her arms and legs crashing against the floor. Cringing at the pain, she automatically tried to scramble onto her hands and knees, knowing she had to get away, knowing Rosie was still coming after her. Terrified, she managed to turn her head back toward the woman.

Or where Rosie should have been.

Jillian froze, her heart thudding in her ears, shock ricocheting through her.

Rosie wasn't there.

The doorway stood empty, gaping with darkness.

Then Jillian heard it, an eternity later, the crack at the bottom of the stairs, the terrible snap, the noise so ugly and horrifying there was no mistaking what it was.

Jillian closed her eyes, bile rising in her throat in horror. No other sound came from the bottom of the stairs.

It was what Rosie had intended for her. Instead, she'd been the one to take that tumble into the basement.

"Jillian!"

And then Adam was there, reaching for her. He gently turned her over onto her back, leaning over her once more. "Are you okay?"

"I think so," she managed to say. "Just… drowsy. Meredith?"

"She's out cold, but I think just sleeping. I need to check on her again."

"Go," she murmured.

"I'm not leaving you here," he said. In one fluid motion, he had her back in his arms. A place, she had to admit, where it felt very good to be.

Holding her close to his chest, he rose to his feet. "Wait," she said when he would have turned away. "I need to see." Had to know for sure.

He paused, allowing her to glance back. Down the stairs.

Rosie lay at the bottom, her head twisted at an unnatural, impossible angle, her eyes staring blankly upward.

"All right," Jillian murmured, already glancing away. She took no pleasure from the sight, only the confirmation that the woman wasn't a threat anymore—and never would be again.

Adam began to turn away again. As he did, she finally saw the person standing behind him.

Ed loomed in the doorway, his large body stiff and menacing.

Jillian tensed in alarm, opening her mouth to call out a warning to Adam.

From the way Adam froze she realized he must have seen him.

His eyes pinned beyond them, Ed slowly moved toward them, his heavily lined face sagging with grief and, most of all, weariness. Adam stepped to the side, and Ed passed them as if they weren't even there. They both watched as he came to a stop at the basement door. Slowly sinking onto the top step, he sat there, staring silently down at the bottom.

After a moment, Adam turned and started toward the door out of the kitchen. Jillian wondered if they should just leave Ed there, if he was still a threat, even as something told her he wasn't. Either way, she couldn't manage to find the words.

Feeling so damnably weak, there was nothing she could do but let Adam hold her to him and carry her from the room. It was enough. More than enough. Relief gradually replacing the adrenaline pumping through her system, she closed her eyes, listening to the sound of his heart pounding, soaking in the strength of his body around her, safe in the knowledge that the long nightmare was finally over.

Chapter Sixteen

The storm finally died down just before dawn. The pouring rain gradually subsided, then tapered off into nothing. The dark, heavy clouds remained, blocking out the rising sun. The world was still shrouded in grayness when the remaining occupants of Sutton Hall came outside to watch the police and the coroner's van drive away.

Ed sat in the back of the police cruiser. He hadn't said a word since Rosie's death. It had taken some time for the police to arrive due to the storm. The whole time Ed had sat quietly at the top of the stairs and watched over his sister's body at the bottom. When the authorities had finally arrived, he'd allowed himself to be handcuffed and gone with them willingly, all without saying anything to explain or defend himself while Jillian and Adam told their stories. As the cruiser finally pulled away, he didn't even look at the people who'd come to watch him go, staring blankly ahead.

"He looks so lost," Meredith murmured.

There was a trace of sympathy in her voice, and in spite of everything, Jillian couldn't help but feel a bit of it herself for the man. "He spent his life taking care of his sister and trying to protect her. I wonder if he even cares what will happen to him now. It must feel like he doesn't have anything left."

Standing next to Meredith, Adam said nothing. Jillian knew he was still angry with the man, but deep down she suspected he had to admit he understood Ed's actions, even if he couldn't excuse them.

"I can't believe I didn't know," Grace murmured faintly, not for the first time. Evidently the Warrens had kept up their pretense to the fullest, even filing their income taxes as a married couple. The only tip-off in retrospect was that they'd asked for twin beds in their room, claiming that Rosie couldn't sleep with all of Ed's tossing and turning at night. They'd never shown much physical affection toward each other, but given the clear tension in their relationship, no one had ever taken that as odd. Otherwise there'd been no other indications they weren't exactly what they'd claimed to be.

The two vehicles slowly headed down the

driveway, finally cresting the curve and disappearing from view.

As soon as they were gone, Ray and Zack stepped off the porch and shuffled off toward the groundskeeper's cottage. It had been a long night for all of them, but for those two in particular, working to curb the damage from the storm in Ed's absence.

Grace lingered a moment longer before silently turning and withdrawing into the house, leaving Jillian standing on the porch with Adam and Meredith.

It was the first time she'd been able to speak with Meredith since she'd found out the truth, and Jillian couldn't help but give her an uneasy glance.

"Meredith," she said, drawing the other woman's attention. "I'm sorry for lying to you. About who I am, why I really came here."

Meredith shook her head. "It's all right. I understand. And if you hadn't lied, we never would have known the truth about what happened and Rosie would have been free to hurt someone else. I'm just sorry it came to that, and that we allowed her to be in a position where she could hurt you and your friend in the first place."

"That's my fault," Adam said roughly. "I should have checked deeper—"

"No," Jillian interrupted. "Unless you're hiring for the government, no standard employment background check is going to dig into people's families and relationships. There's no reasonable way you could have known. They've been living this charade for twenty-five years and found a way to pull it off and cover their tracks." She swallowed. "And even if I had been here, I probably couldn't have saved Courtney. I wouldn't have been with her all the time, so Rosie would have been able to come through the passages and get to her in her room when she was alone anyway. So no more blaming ourselves for things we couldn't reasonably control. Any of us."

"Agreed," Meredith said pointedly, looking at Adam long and hard.

Adam met her gaze with surprising vulnerability, and it was clear he knew exactly what she was talking about. She was releasing him from the burden he felt he owed her. His strong face softened with such love for his sister that Jillian melted a little inside. Finally, he nodded.

Jillian turned to Meredith. "And now that it's over, you can make a go of your wedding business for real."

A sad smile touched Meredith's lips. "Somehow I doubt anyone will want to get married here now. It was bad enough when everyone thought a bride had accidentally died here. Now that we know it was murder, who would want to come here?"

"You never know." Jillian leaned back and gazed up at the building. "This is still an amazing place. I have to believe a lot of people would love to see it. I'm sure you could manage to find some way to make it work. If not for weddings, then something else. Maybe all it needs is a fresh start." She smiled. "Sometimes that's all any of us needs."

Meredith nodded slightly. "I can't argue with that." Her gaze suddenly shifted from Jillian to Adam and back again, her lips curving knowingly. "It's been a long night. I think I'm going to try to get some sleep. I'll see you both later." Without waiting for a response, Meredith slipped into the house.

And Jillian was finally alone with Adam.

A tremor of anticipation rumbled through her. This was the first time they'd really had a chance to talk since he'd taken her into his arms after Rosie's death.

The first time they'd been completely alone since they'd made love in his office.

"Thank you for that," Adam said softly.

"I meant it," Jillian said. "You have something good started here. It would be a shame to give up on it so quickly without giving it a chance."

Only when the words came out did she realize how they sounded, as though she was talking about something else.

Or maybe she was, she acknowledged, as she breathed in the sight of him standing before her, her heart beating faster in response.

Adam eyed her seriously. "Now that you know what really happened to Courtney here, I imagine you'd want to get away from this place as fast as you can."

"It's not the place's fault." Jillian pictured Courtney the way she liked to remember her best, smiling, always smiling, and she knew Courtney must have done plenty of that here. "And while it will always be connected to her death, I'll always remember how excited she was to be here. She loved it, too."

A lump rose in her throat when she thought of Courtney, so excited, preparing for her wedding. Whatever else had happened, her last days had been happy ones.

Suddenly she felt his arms go around her. She closed her eyes and leaned into him, savoring his strength, his warmth.

"I know," he said softly. "I remember. You're right. She was excited to be here. And very happy."

"Thank *you* for that," she murmured against his chest.

"I really wouldn't blame you if you wanted to leave as fast as you can."

It wasn't a suggestion. He wasn't pushing her to go. Indeed, he actually sounded pained by the idea, unable to completely keep the resignation from his voice. But he was saying it for her sake. Because he thought it was what she needed, what would make her happy. That was who he was.

And it reminded her exactly why she should stay.

Jillian leaned back and peered up into his face. "I'm not going anywhere. I think there's a lot more here that's worth exploring further."

One corner of his mouth began to curve upward. Hope, excitement, relief flared in those fascinating eyes. "Oh, you do?"

"I do." She smiled. "Haven't you learned by now it's not that easy to get rid of me?"

"Then I guess it's a good thing I no longer want to."

"Like that would stop me."

He threw his head back and laughed. "You really are impossible."

"It's a good thing you like that about me."

And he smiled, the sight of it there on that

lean, chiseled, beautiful face making her heart lurch in her chest and start pounding faster. "I like a lot more than that about you."

"I'm glad to hear it."

He started to pull her close again. Before he could entirely, she stayed him with a hand on his chest. "Oh, and one thing."

"What is it?"

"Let's take things slow. I'm not sure I'm going to be up for planning a wedding anytime soon."

He laughed. "Understood. Like you said, I think there's plenty for us to explore before then."

As she took in the beauty of his smile and the warmth of his features, she wondered how she could have ever thought him cold.

Unable to resist any longer, she wrapped her arms around him.

As she clung to him, a bright light suddenly washed over her, the glow glaring through her eyelids. She opened them slightly to find the sun had finally managed to break through the clouds, shining its warmth upon them.

And on Sutton Hall.

Turning her head to rest it on Adam's shoulder, she looked up at the building. She saw no shadows in its windows and many corners, the light filling every nook and crevice. Its walls still wet from the rain, the whole manor seemed to gleam, clean and fresh once more in the bright light of morning.

A new day had begun at Sutton Hall at last.

* * * * *

Look for Meredith's story next month as Kerry Connor's miniseries
SUTTON HALL WEDDINGS *concludes in*
THE BEST MAN TO TRUST,
only from Harlequin Intrigue!

LARGER-PRINT BOOKS!
GET 2 FREE LARGER-PRINT NOVELS PLUS
2 FREE GIFTS!

◆ HARLEQUIN®

INTRIGUE®

BREATHTAKING ROMANTIC SUSPENSE

HILPI3R

ReaderService.com

Manage your account online!

- Review your order history
- Manage your payments
- Update your address

> **We've designed
> the Harlequin® Reader Service
> website just for you.**

Enjoy all the features!

- Reader excerpts from any series
- Respond to mailings and
  special monthly offers
- Discover new series available to you
- Browse the Bonus Bucks catalog
- Share your feedback

Visit us at:

ReaderService.com

RS13